GOODBYE, MY LOVER

by

Victor J. Banis

The Borgo Press
An Imprint of Wildside Press

MMVII

SECOND EDITION

CONTENTS

◊

CHAPTER ONE
◇

"Sure looks big from up here, doesn't it?"

Lost for the moment in his own thoughts, Dennis Eastman started at the sound of the voice and turned his head to look at the speaker sitting next to him on the plane.

"I'm sorry," he said apologetically. "I was thinking. What did you say?"

"The city, Los Angeles," his neighbor said, nodding his head in the direction of the airplane's window. "I said, it looks awfully big from up here, doesn't it?"

"Oh, yes, I guess it does," Dennis agreed without interest. In fact, although he had been staring from the window, he had paid little attention to Los Angeles, sprawled for what seemed endless miles beneath them. His thoughts had been far removed from his surroundings.

"Of course, it actually is very big, enormous, in fact," the stranger persisted. "Is this your first trip here to Los Angeles?"

Dennis looked back at him, sizing the man up rapidly: he was middle-aged, slightly plump, beginning to lose his hair—and, he was definitely homosexual, which no doubt accounted for his attempts to establish a conversation, particularly now that they were nearing their mutual destination. No doubt he was hoping for a further acquaintance with the young man seated next to him.

"No, I've been here before," Dennis answered the question, resigning himself to the demands of courtesy. Rudeness was a trait he had never developed, sometimes to his regret. It would be far easier simply to turn away from the speaker, terminate the conversation now and completely. He wouldn't, of course; he would only resent the intrusion upon his privacy.

"Are you here on vacation?" The stranger was plainly encouraged by his response, warming up to the situation as he thought it had developed.

Dennis considered the question briefly. "I guess you could say so," he said aloud.

Vacation? Could you really call it that, he wondered? It was true, he was on leave, with almost a full thirty days left before he returned east, returned to the Naval Academy to begin his education there. But, vacation implied, in his mind, something different from this trip. It suggested an idle journey, with little purpose beyond relaxation and enjoyment, and while he would surely experience some enjoyment while he was here, there was definitely a purpose to his trip, a purpose beyond pleasure, that was of considerable importance to him, and that had occupied his thoughts for some time now, that had kept him staring out the airplane's window, seeing nothing.

The plane was passing low over a racetrack—Hollywood Park, he thought it was called—and would be landing soon. The light had come on to warn the passengers to fasten their seat belts. Dennis did so, at the same time putting his cigarette out in the ashtray.

Just a few more minutes, only minutes before he saw Linc once more, before he came face to face with decisions that he should have long since made, made before he even set out on this trip.

He became aware that the man sitting next to him had spoken again, was looking at him, waiting for an answer. He thought back, trying to recall what the question might have been.

"You are lost in the clouds, aren't you?" The man chuckled, ignoring the seatbelt sign. "I asked if I could give you a lift when we got in, or is someone meeting you?"

"Thanks, but someone is meeting me," Dennis said.

The stranger's disappointment was obvious and for a moment or two his attempts at conversation faltered.

Yes, Dennis repeated to himself silently, someone is meeting me all right. Linc, Lincoln Gardner, would be waiting when he got off the plane, his intense eyes scanning the passengers deplaning, his face coming to radiant life as he recognized the right face, the one he was searching for. A few women in the crowd would almost certainly glance around hurriedly but with admiration at the tall, handsome man, perhaps flatter themselves that his eager glances were for them. They would never suspect the truth, never guess that the clean-cut, youthful man Linc was meeting was the real object of his desire. He would not show his desire, of course, not there in the airport. That would come out later, back in Linc's apartment, when the two of them were alone. Thinking of what would happen then, Dennis could feel already his own desire stir with his tensing thighs.

He shuddered and tried to force the thought from his mind, but it returned. Yes, it was true: the desire was on his part as well. He could not delude himself about that. For a year he had tried to convince himself otherwise, tried to make himself believe that it had been only a matter of circumstances.

The circumstances had played their part: that was true enough. He had known Linc all of his life, for one thing. Their families had always been close; their fathers long time friends, although the age difference between himself and Linc had for years prevented their being really close. Linc, after all, was nearly fifteen years older. He had been nearly thirty when Dennis was only a fifteen-year-old boy. Yet it was strange that the age difference had seemed so much less five years later. Twenty and thirty-five had seemed far closer than fifteen and thirty, and they had discovered in one another new friends.

It was natural enough that, on the death of his father, Dennis and his mother should have come to California, to stay for a time with their friends, the Gardners; and it was natural, too, that Dennis should have turned to Linc, an older man for companionship; a man not too many years younger than his own father had been.

It had all been quite natural: the long days together at the beach or in the mountains, the nights of listening to music or talking for long hours about poetry and literature. Linc had awakened his own innate interest in the arts, and they had never lacked for things to talk about or do.

It had been just as natural that Dennis should begin to stay over at Linc's apartment. After all, he was spending most of his time there anyway. For most of the time that Dennis was in California, the two of them talked together, ate together, slept together, even showered together. What had finally happened between them was probably as inevitable as it was natural.

The difficulties had not come until later, until Dennis' leave was ended and he had returned to the Naval base. It was then that he had time to think about what had happened and his thoughts were influenced by the remarks that he heard from the other sailors, remarks about "queers," and "fairies." Dennis had come to realize, without fully understanding it, that his comrades were talking about him. Not that they knew, about him specifically; but, gradually, he had come to know, to see himself through their eyes. He hadn't liked what he saw.

He had seen Linc after that, of course. His mother was still in California, they could well afford that Dennis spend his leaves there, flying back and forth across the country. Nor did his mother question the fact that she rarely saw her son on those weekends. He was inevitably with Linc.

Each visit had been harder, each time the guilt and uncertainties greater. "I love you," Linc had insisted. "Nothing else matters."

It had mattered, though. It had mattered that Dennis could not believe those words, nor say them himself. How could two men love one another, he wondered? Friendship, yes, and physical gratification, certainly they shared that between them by this time; but, not love.

Still, Linc had remained confident, so much so that he had agreed to the year. One year, Dennis had asked for, a year apart, not seeing one another at all. That would give them—him, particularly—the time to think, to consider the relationship for what it was. Hopefully, although he had not told Linc this, time to discover that it was unimportant to him.

What was he going to tell Linc, now that the year was over? That he had tried to forget it all? That he had dated countless young girls back East, satisfying himself sexually with many of them? Was he going to tell him that the desire for Linc was still there, unrelieved by his other experiences, no matter how many; that the unnamed emotion that he still could not classify was there as well?

After his year, he still did not know the answers. He was here, in California, as they had agreed. He had his leave, thirty days of it, and he had come to spend it with Linc. Beyond that, he was as confused and uncertain as ever.

The man beside him gave Dennis a final glance as he rose from his seat, hopeful but not confident. Dennis nodded curtly and stood also, reaching for his jacket on the shelf above the seats.

He stood five-ten, his body compact and taut. Tan Levis fitted snugly to slender hips and solid, powerful looking limbs. His shoulders were wide, and above them his face was good looking in an almost childish way, dominated by wide eyes of a startling green and topped off by a shock of white-blond hair that insisted upon tumbling across his forehead. He was, in fact, far better looking than he realized, and his lack of conceit only enhanced his youthful appeal.

Flinging the jacket casually over one shoulder, he made his way toward the front of the plane, past the stewardess whose smile brightened as she saw him, and down the tunnel-like ramp.

He paused as he entered the waiting room, glancing about at the people waiting to meet passengers. A pair of eyes met his, dropped downward to pause at the point where his Levis bulged noticeably outward in the front, and made their way back up.

Dennis looked quickly away, blushing. The smiling, masculine face was not Linc's, but another man's, a stranger's. Linc was not there.

He must have gotten tied up in traffic, Dennis thought. Probably Linc would be there by the time he had picked up his bag. He walked rapidly past the smiling stranger and made his way to the escalator that took him to the main lobby. His bag appeared shortly, carried along on a conveyer belt. He removed it, set it aside, and scanned the crowd once more. Still no sign of Linc.

It was unlike Linc to be late for anything, certainly strange that he should have been late today. Lighting a cigarette with hands that, to his annoyance, were trembling slightly, Dennis took his bag with him and crossed the lobby to the row of telephone booths.

There was no answer at Linc's apartment. Nor was there any message for him at the information counter. He seated himself on one of the plastic leather benches near the entrance door and waited, smoking another cigarette as quickly as he finished the first one.

Something must have happened; maybe an accident. He shook his head, dismissing that idea. Whatever it was, it was probably something very silly and trivial, the sort of thing that could not be foreseen. Still, Linc could have phoned or at least left a message for him.

Maybe after all Linc had changed his mind. Maybe the year had been sufficient for him to see that he wasn't so "in love" as he thought. Maybe he had found someone else. The books that Dennis had read all said homosexuals were unstable, fickle people.

With an impatient gesture, he dropped his cigarette to the floor, crushing it beneath his foot, and stood. He was accomplishing nothing sitting here stewing like this. He had a key to Linc's apartment after all. There was nothing to prevent his going there, and if Linc missed him here at the airport, he would certainly go back there.

"Miss your friend?"

Dennis turned to face his companion from the airplane, once more hopeful and smiling.

"He got tied up," Dennis lied without knowing why he should bother to offer any explanation to this stranger.

"I can give you a lift," the man offered.

Dennis stared at him for a moment. It would do no harm to accept the offer. The man would make a pass, of course, but he had only to refuse. For that matter, what harm would there be if he accepted....

"No, thanks," he said rather curtly. He walked past the man and out the door, heading for a taxicab parked a short distance away.

* * * * * * *

Alone, in the back seat of the taxi, Dennis forced himself to concentrate on the passing scenery, shutting out the increasingly troublesome thoughts that attempted to crowd into his mind.

It was January, only a scant few days after the beginning of the New Year. The weather in the east was still cold and unpleasant. He had never gotten over the thrill of flying into California during this season. It was like waking from the night's sleep to be greeted by the sunlight of morning, or stepping from a dark room into a lighted one. Here everything was green and brilliant, the late afternoon sun golden and warm. Flowers bloomed profusely in the lawns bordering the Spanish-style homes, and the teen-age girls along the streets were in shorts or other skimpy summer attire.

The neighborhood began to change, the homes becoming larger and more ornate. A sign announced that they were entering Beverly Hills, and a few minutes later they were pulling up to the curb outside the apartment building. Dennis thrust a ten-dollar bill into the driver's hand, waving away the change, and suppressed a desire to dash up the steps, forcing himself instead to walk slowly and casually into the lobby.

He paused at the door of Linc's apartment and, on an impulse, rang the bell. It had occurred to him that it was possible Linc was with someone else. It would be embarrassing if he just barged in.

There was no answer and he unlocked the door with his key, closing it nervously after himself. The apartment seemed close and stuffy, and a glance around showed him that all the windows were closed.

"Linc?" he called. There was no answer. He left his bag by the door and crossed to one of the tall French doors that opened onto the balcony and opened it wide to let some fresh air into the room. It was probably only a false impression, but it seemed to him that the room had been closed up longer than a few hours.

That's not entirely out of the question, he thought. He had written Linc to tell him he was coming and to give him the time of his arrival and the flight number, but he had not waited to receive a reply. What if Linc were out of town, and hadn't gotten his letter? That would explain why Linc hadn't met him at the airport or left him a message.

He went to the kitchen and opened the refrigerator. The bread on the lower shelf was still fresh. So was the quart of milk that he opened and sniffed. No, if Linc was gone, he had only been gone a couple of days, no longer. The letter should have arrived over the weekend, and it was Wednesday now.

Of course, Linc might have written to him, to explain that he wouldn't be available today. He had been gone from the base since the end of the previous week, going from there into New York, where he had done some shopping and allowed himself the privilege of putting off the reunion for another day or two.

A scrap of paper on the kitchen counter caught his eye. He picked it up, thinking it might be a note from Linc, but it was only a shopping list. He returned it to the counter, and then picked it up again, studying it more closely. There was nothing particularly unusual about the list—a few grocery items, a type of photographic developing solution, cigarettes—but the handwriting was not Linc's. It could have been written, he supposed, by the day-maid who cleaned for him, but the cigarettes were not Linc's old brand. He could have changed brands, of course, but so far as he knew, Linc had never had any interest in photography.

It had become increasingly clear to him: Linc had not waited the year after all. There was already someone else living in the apartment.

"I should be glad," Dennis told himself. This saved him the necessity of making a decision, spared them a difficult scene. Only, he wasn't glad at all. He felt as though someone had just dealt him a violent blow in the pit of his stomach, knocking the wind out of him.

He jumped when the doorbell ran. Linc's new friend, he wondered? Should he answer it, or ignore it and leave when the coast was clear? The bell rang again, insistently.

Disappointment turning into anger, Dennis strode rapidly through the living room to the front door, flinging it open. *Let's just see*, he told himself.

The man facing him was a stranger, although he hardly seemed at a glance to be Linc's type. He was older than Linc, nice looking, but in a hardened way. Only his eyes held any trace of warmth or kindness, and they were studying Dennis now in a manner that was hard to read.

"You're Dennis Eastman," the visitor greeted him, more as though stating a fact known to both of them than as though asking a question.

"Yes," Dennis answered simply, making no attempt to invite the man inside. It was possible that this was someone else, a business associate perhaps, although he was puzzled by the fact that the stranger knew his name.

"Sergeant Mathews," the stranger explained, opening his billfold to reveal a badge pinned inside it. "Beverly Hills Police."

Dennis stepped back automatically, allowing entrance to the apartment. Was Linc in some trouble with the police? He wasn't the type to get himself picked up for public misbehavior, he was too discreet for that, but there were always things that could happen. Homosexuals were vulnerable in many ways.

"Sorry no one met you at the airport, but I figured it might be a little awkward for you," the policeman said, leading the way into the living room. "Besides, I figured you would be coming here right off."

"Is there some sort of trouble?" Dennis asked.

"Quite a bit." Sergeant Mathews looked around and motioned toward the sofa. "Have a seat."

"Thanks," Dennis answered, seating himself gratefully on the sofa. The Sergeant sat on one of the chairs facing the sofa, on the edge of the seat, and stared at him quietly for a long moment before going on.

"Lincoln Gardner is dead," Mathews told him finally.

The room seemed to spin. Instinctively Dennis clutched at the arm of the sofa as though he might at any moment be flung into space. "Dead?" he repeated dazedly, not quite able to comprehend.

"He was murdered, two nights ago, here in this room—shot, to be exact. Are you okay?"

Dennis shook his head, unable for the moment to speak. He fought to retain control of himself. Linc, murdered? Surely it wasn't possible. These things didn't happen, not to real people, people that you knew. You read about them in the newspapers or saw them in movies, but they never really affected you; they never happened to Linc Gardner.

"If you're worried about me," Sergeant Mathews was saying from a great distance away, "About me being a cop, I mean, I already know about the two of you."

Dennis shook his head again, trying to jar his mind into functioning. Later, there would be time to feel, to grieve, but not now, in front of this stranger, this man who had never known Linc, who was never in Linc's arms.... "You know about us?"

"Gardner kept diaries," Mathews said. "I had to read them. You're Dennis Eastman, from the Baltimore Eastmans. Good family, well off. You're in the Navy, like your father and all of his family.

17

You've known Lincoln Gardner for years. The two of you had a little fling together a year or so ago. You wrote to him last week, telling him you'd be here today."

Sergeant Mathews removed the letter from his pocket and tossed it on to the table between them. Dennis left it there with no more than a glance. It was certainly his letter. He could see that.

"Am I under arrest?" he asked instead. It was still hard to understand all this. He was only beginning to make sense out of what the policeman was telling him.

Sergeant Mathews shook his head and smiled for the first time, not an unpleasant smile. "If I had wanted to do that, I could have had you picked up at your base, or at your home."

"I was in New York."

"You stayed at the Wilton. Oh, I checked on you, but don't worry about it. I was careful, I didn't cause you any problems, or say anything that would come back to embarrass you. With any kind of luck, your name will never make it to print."

"Thanks, I appreciate that." Dennis lit a cigarette, inhaling deeply. All his energies were directed at remaining calm, thinking clearly.

"Don't quote me on this, it would look bad for the department, my saying it, but I don't really care what the two of you did together. I'm not saying I think it was smart of either of you, but it doesn't enter into my case. The important thing to me is that you didn't kill Gardner."

"Of course I didn't," Dennis snapped. The gray eyes were still watching him closely. He raised his own to meet them. "Who did?" he asked in a small voice.

Mathews sighed and shook his head again. 'I don't know that," he said. "Do you want to hear about it?"

Dennis nodded, unable to trust his voice. Mathews stood and walked to the window, turning his back on Dennis as he spoke.

"It's not much of a mystery how he died, or why. It was just the sort of thing that happens from time to time with…with you people. He was in a bar Monday night, not a very nice one. It's called The Ship's Call."

"A…a gay bar?" Dennis had difficulty even saying the word. He had never used it in reference to himself or Linc.

Mathews nodded, glancing back over his shoulder. "It's mostly a hangout for the leather set, in Hollywood," he said. "Like I said, it's not a very nice place. Your friend came in early, about eight-thirty. He picked up a kid there and left with him about nine."

Dennis tried to sort out his thoughts. Linc, in a bar of that sort? Linc, who had disapproved of gay bars in general, of pickups like that, who had in-sisted that it didn't have to be like that for two men who loved one another?

"He picked up the wrong trick, apparently," Mathews went on. "They came here, we know that much. They had a drink, very good Scotch, I'd say. Gardner played the piano for him, entertainment, I suppose, or maybe to set the mood. That was about eleven when the neighbors heard him playing the piano. The maid found him dead when she came to clean the next morning."

Mathews had turned from the window and was watching him, as if waiting for some comment. Dennis sat in silence, trying to imagine the scene being enacted, but the images refused to come. It was too unlike Linc. Nothing would fit with the Linc that he remembered.

"It's not an unusual case, like I said," Mathews went on. "From the description we got, the guy he picked up was pretty rough looking—rough trade, I think you guys call them. He had his fun, robbed your buddy, and killed him. Not much of a mystery, except who the guy was, and we'll find him soon enough."

Still Dennis said nothing. He had finished his cigarette and now he lit another, staring blankly ahead of him.

"Got any ideas that might help us?" Mathews asked him.

Dennis shook his head. "It's not like Linc—Lincoln. He didn't go to those places, he wouldn't have gone for that type of person."

There was a long moment of silence. "Maybe he had changed," Mathews said finally. "You've been away a while."

Dennis fell silent again. He couldn't expect this man to know, to understand. To him it was a "clear case," the sort of thing that happened from time to time to "you people."

"Is that yours?" Mathew asked him.

Dennis followed his gaze and realized finally that he was still carrying the shopping list he had found in the kitchen.

20

"No," he answered, glancing at the list again. "I found it in the kitchen."

"I left it there," Mathews explained. "That's where we found it. It's not Gardner's handwriting."

"No, it isn't." Dennis put the list on the coffee table. "Do you think…?"

"It doesn't seem like the sort of thing a murderer would leave behind, particularly a young punk like the one we're looking for. Some friend may have left it here, maybe even weeks ago. One other thing: do you know any friends of Gardner's named Jeff?"

Dennis thought for a moment, trying to recall the year before. Their time had mostly been spent together, just the two of them. There were one or two friends of Linc's that he remembered quite clearly, some he had gotten to know fairly well.

"I don't think so," he said after a moment, "But he had an address book. He kept it in the den."

He started to rise, but Mathews shook his head. "We checked that already," he said, "but there's no Jeff in it. The name was written on a note pad, by the phone. It might be a clue, or at least a lead, or it might mean nothing."

Mathews went across the room, toward the door. "I guess maybe you would like me to get out of here and leave you alone," he said.

Dennis stood, following him to the door. "Is there anything I should do?" he asked.

"No. Stay around town for a few days, in case I come up with any questions. I don't think it will take us too long to find the guy."

"Of course," Dennis said. "I'll be staying here in Linc's…Mister Gardner's apartment for a few days, at least. That is, of course, if it's all right with you."

"We have no objections, I'm sure," Mathews said. "I'll check in at headquarters just to make sure, but the crime scene techs have finished their work, and the rent's paid for the month, at least, so I can't see any reason why you shouldn't stay for a bit."

"Thank you. I appreciate your kindness, and if there's anything I can do, just call on me. I just hope I can be of some help to you."

"I'll keep in touch," Mathews said. He opened the door and paused briefly. "His funeral's tomorrow, by the way," he said before he left, closing the door after himself.

CHAPTER TWO

◊

In the distance a group of tourists had paused in their wanderings to stare in the direction of the burial service. The area around the gravesite was banked with flowers, their myriad colors bright and garish in the sunlight. The horn of a car sounded somewhere in the distance.

Dennis stood stiffly beside his mother. He heard her start to cry again and automatically pulled his handkerchief from his pocket, handing it to her wordlessly.

Dennis scarcely listened to the words that the minister was saying, nor would he allow himself to cry. He had done that the evening before, long after Mathews had gone. There had been the call to the Gardners, and the news that his mother was on her way; then the trip to the airport, and apologies for the fact that his mother had not been able to get in touch with him. She had checked into a hotel and, finally, much later, he had returned to Linc's apartment. At last, there had been time to cry, lying in the bed that he had once shared with Linc, remembering Linc's arms about him, the hungry eagerness of Linc's body against his.

It was over at last. Dennis waited with his mother until the elder Gardners had left. He promised them that they would stop by their house to see them. Then he led his mother to the car he had rented.

He drove mechanically, leaving the cemetery behind them and making his way into the frenzied afternoon traffic of the Los Angeles freeway system.

"It's so hard to believe," his mother said sadly, still sniffing into the handkerchief. "He was always so alive, don't you think?"

Dennis bit his lip savagely and left the question unanswered. He couldn't very well say, yes, Linc had been so alive, he had been so warm and hard, and so hungry for your son's body. He couldn't say that.

The Gardner estate was in Bel Air, sprawled over a gently rolling hill, a large, regal home that had been something of a showplace when the Gardners had been younger. They were both well on in years now; Linc had been born to them late in life, their first and their last child. With his birth, their attention had been devoted to him and there had been little need or use for the large home or its sweeping grounds. Some of the land had been sold off and a great deal of the house was closed up. The funeral parlor, Linc had called it, preferring the comfort of his more modern apartment. In the end, though, as Dennis reminded himself, it was the apartment that had been the funeral parlor.

24

The Gardner maid, only slightly younger than Emma Gardner herself, showed them into the parlor. Mrs. Gardner joined them there a moment later, wearing a brightly patterned robe that was too young for her and had the effect of making her appear all the more aged and drawn.

"I sent Henry to bed," she apologized for her husband's absence. "His heart's bad, you know, and all this excitement hasn't been good for him. I've expected a stroke for three days now. Have some sherry with me, please."

She poured the wine with trembling hands and gave the Eastmans their glasses. "You don't know how awful it's been," she said, "The things they have tried to say. Why, the police even hinted that Lincoln was homosexual."

Dennis' heart pounded loudly in his chest, but she went on without a pause, "And you of all people, Dennis, know how silly that is. But I warned them. I told them that if one word of that sort of thing got into the papers, heads would roll. The Gardner name still carries weight around this town, they won't likely forget that."

"But how *did* it happen, Emma?" Mrs. Eastman asked over the rim of her glass. "I couldn't make any sense at all out of the newspaper reports."

"Robbery," Mrs. Gardner answered confidently. "Plain old unadulterated robbery. If those police would only listen to what one tells them, they'd make things easier for themselves. I've tried at least three times to tell them about the money, and I swear I don't think they had the vaguest idea what I was talking about."

"Money? What money?" Dennis asked. Nothing had been mentioned to him about money.

"The money Linc had. He had drawn two thousand dollars out of the bank not three days before, and not a penny of it has showed up. Now, I know Linc was sometimes extravagant with money, but he just could not have spent that much in three days, and if he did, what did he spend it on?"

Dennis thought about that question while the two women talked on. What could Linc have spent that much money on? There was nothing in the apartment that he recognized as new. Of course, it might have gone for clothes, but Linc's wardrobe had been extensive to begin with. He would hardly need to add that much to it. A car? No, Linc's Mercedes, an older, classic one ninety, was still in the garage at the apartment building. He had seen it just this morning.

Two thousand dollars—that was ample motive for murder—but it still didn't explain the bar, or why Linc, with his culture and sensitivity, would have been interested in a young hoodlum wearing a leather jacket, one of the motorcycle crowd; a far cry from the circle of friends Linc had enjoyed and cultivated in the past. A motorcyclist named Jeff?

"We'd better be going," Mrs. Eastman said, standing. Dennis rose also.

"I've been staying at the apartment," Dennis said to Mrs. Gardner. It had occurred to him only this morning that, in fact, he had no right to the apartment. He had never been anything more than Linc's guest—and Linc was no longer there.

"Oh, do stay on there, as long as you like," Mrs. Gardner insisted, clasping his hand warmly.

"Linc would have wanted you to. He was quite fond of you, you know. He said you were like a little brother to him."

Dennis smiled gratefully. "I'd like to stay, for a few days, at least. And I thought a lot of Linc, too, I assure you."

"Oh, dear, wait one moment." Mrs. Gardner went out of the room and came back a minute later, carrying a large manila envelope bulging with odd shapes. She handed it to Dennis.

"These were Linc's things," she said, "The things he had on him when, when they found him. Take them with you, please. His keys are here, and you'll want them. You know his car, and I am sure he would want you to use it while you are here. Please don't hesitate."

Dennis thanked her again and they left. He dropped his mother at her hotel, declining the suggestion to have dinner with her, pleading the need for some time alone to deal with his grief, and drove directly back to Linc's apartment.

The envelope contained Linc's billfold, but the money was gone from it, although his assailant had neglected to take his expensive watch and the ring with its large, exquisitely cut emerald. That in itself was worth two thousand dollars, maybe more. The thief, if that was what he had been, had been rather a shortsighted one, it seemed. The keys were there, as Mrs. Gardner had said, on a ring. There were only three of them, two for the car and one for the apartment. He left them on the chest near the front door and went into the kitchen to pour himself a tall drink of Chivas.

Seated on the sofa again, sipping the Scotch, he let his mind go back to the murder. He had tried to fit the pieces together, tried to accept the story Mathews had given him, but it didn't fit. Nothing rang true.

He wondered if Mathews knew about the money. Mrs. Gardner said she had tried to tell the police about it, but she was inclined to be a little scatterbrained under the best of circumstances. She might have been incomprehensible when she talked to the police. Perhaps he should call Mathews and tell him about the money—but what would that prove? Mathews would regard it as corroboration of his theory, wouldn't he? Tempted by the money, the unknown visitor had lost his head and killed Linc. Frightened by what he had done, he might logically have overlooked the other valuables, or he might have considered them too easy to trace.

What about the name, Jeff? Did that really mean anything? If Jeff was the murderer, then he was probably someone Linc had known before the night he met him at the bar. Linc was most certainly not the sort to bring a stranger back to his apartment. It was just too out of character. Perhaps Linc had gone to the bar to meet him. That would explain Linc's presence in such an unlikely place; but it still left Linc's interest in Jeff unexplained.

Of course, he had been away for a year, as Mathews had reminded him. Perhaps Linc had changed. Maybe he had grown bored with the sophisticated and the polished, and had been tempted by the thrill of a dangerously crude and perhaps very attractive young man.

He heard the sound of a key in the front door lock. Dennis jumped to his feet, spilling his drink. For an instant he had raced back in time, he was waiting here for Linc to come home; but it wasn't Linc at the door, of course. That wasn't possible. Mathews? No, Mathews had rung the bell when he had been here before. He wasn't the sort to let himself in without ringing first.

Dennis heart seemed to stop in his chest. Or was he about to come face to face with the mysterious young man in leather—Linc's murderer?

* * * * * * *

It was not the mysterious stranger who opened the door, and stepped into the apartment, however, but rather a face from the past.

"Frank Davenport," Dennis said his name aloud, feeling both disappointed and relieved at the same time.

"Dennis!" Davenport was plainly as surprised at the encounter as Dennis was. He stood just inside the door, his hand on the knob, and for a second he looked so shaken that Dennis half expected him to turn and run.

"This is a surprise," Frank said finally, coming into the room and closing the door. "I didn't know you were back in town."

"I got in just yesterday afternoon," Dennis said.

"You know about...?"

Dennis nodded his head. "I found out when I got here. But what are you doing here, at the apartment, I mean? You have your own key?"

"Oh, the key?" Frank laughed as he glanced down at the key in his hand. "Linc gave it to me several months ago. I was having some work done on my place, and he told me to use his when I liked. The thing is, I left a pair of cuff links here a while back, and I've been wanting to come by to get them when the police weren't around."

"I see." It seemed to Dennis that Frank was acting strangely; but then, he and Frank have never gotten along very well. He was probably letting his imagination run away with him. "Can I offer you a drink?" he asked.

"Love one. Scotch, please, on the rocks." He sat on the sofa and waited in the living room while Dennis went into the kitchen to get the drink. From the other room he heard the rattle of ice being emptied into a bowl. "You're staying here, in the apartment?" he asked.

"While I'm on leave," Dennis said, coming back into the room with the drink and seating himself across from Frank. "For a couple of weeks, at least."

Frank was silent for a minute or two, sipping at his drink. "I guess this must have been quite a shock for you," he said finally.

"Yes, it was, to say the least. Did I miss you, by the way, at the funeral?"

Frank shook his head. "I couldn't go," he said. "I just couldn't bear seeing him...you understand?"

Dennis left the question unanswered. It was entirely Frank's business whether or not he wanted to attend the funeral. Still, it seemed strange. Frank and Linc had been friends for many years, almost

their entire lives. They had gone to high school together, and later studied music at the same conservatory. He hadn't thought of it at the time, hadn't
even noticed that Frank wasn't there, but now that
he did think of it, it struck him as odd that Frank
should have been absent.

"Dennis," Frank interrupted his thoughts,
"This is a bad time, I know, but, well, you and I
didn't exactly hit it off in the past. We both know
that. I never thought you were right for Linc, with
the difference in age and all, but now I feel pretty
badly about that. I want you to know, I don't dislike
you. I never did. I'd like to be your friend. I think
Linc would want me to try. I think he would want
you to try, too. After all, we were the two people
closest to him."

Dennis face was expressionless, but he did
nevertheless feel some surprise at the gesture. In the
past, Frank had never made a secret of his animos-
ity. Still, what he said was true. Surely Linc would
not want them to be enemies, not now.

"I don't hold any grudges," he said aloud. "I
can see how you felt the way you did. Now, though,
that's all moot, isn't it?"

Frank nodded, seeming to think that settled
the point. "I guess you know about the murder, how
it happened and all that?" he asked.

"I talked to Sergeant Mathews," Dennis said.
"He gave me his version of what happened."

Frank raised one eyebrow quizzically. "You
sound dubious," he said.

Dennis shrugged. "Maybe I am. I don't know
yet exactly what I do think. There are a lot of questions in my mind."

31

Frank studied him while he lit a cigarette. "What story did Mathews give you?" he asked.

"Probably the same one he gave you," Dennis said. "Linc went to some sleazy gay bar, a leather bar, called The Ship's Call, and picked up the wrong trick, a rough looking leather boy, and brought him back here, and things went wrong. The trick killed him, over money or just out of queer hatred. It just doesn't sound like Linc, any of it. You know as well as I do how he felt about gay bars in general, and The Ship's Call sounds like the last place he would have visited, or picked up a trick from. And, a leather boy? I wouldn't have said that was his taste."

Frank looked away from him, toying with the glass in his hands. "You've been away for a while, Dennis," he said simply.

"That's what Mathews told me, too," Dennis said. "People do change, of course, I'm not so young that I don't know that. Tell me, Frank, had Linc changed?"

Frank looked up slowly, his eyes sad. "Yes, Dennis, he had changed."

"In what way?"

"In just the way you're talking about, or ways. I'm sorry, maybe it would be better if you didn't know about it, but you did ask. He was running around with a pretty rough crowd. He had been for months. We even had words about it. I told him time and time again, that he would get into trouble hanging around those places, dating the fellows he was dating. I'm sorry that it turned out I was right. I wish I had been wrong, believe me."

Dennis fought down a wave of angry resentment. Frank was right. He had asked, and he was grateful for the truth, no matter how unpleasant. Still, it was painful hearing these things.

"Then you think it was the way the police described it?" he asked.

Frank nodded. "Frankly, I expected something like this, only not quite so final; but I can't honestly say I was altogether surprised when it did happen like this."

"I see." They sat in silence for a few minutes. "There were some other things that didn't seem to add up," Dennis said.

"Such as?"

"A grocery list in somebody else's handwriting, for one thing, that was left on the kitchen counter."

To his surprise, Frank chuckled aloud. "I'm afraid that's not much of a clue. I left that there myself, a week or so ago."

Dennis got up and retrieved the list from the desk drawer where he had put it. "This one?" he asked.

"The same." Frank took the list and shoved it into a pocket. Dennis briefly considered asking for it back. Really, though, it was of no value now to him, or to anyone else—certainly not the police.

"What else?" Frank asked.

"There was a name, written on a pad by the phone. Do you know if Linc had any friends named Jeff?"

"Jeff?" Frank screwed up his face thoughtfully. "Not that I know of," he said finally. "I'm afraid I can't help you there. Bear in mind, though, that I knew hardly any of these new friends of his. They weren't my type."

It was still difficult for Dennis to believe that they were Linc's type, either. He sat back down again. "I don't know," he said, "It still just doesn't ring true with me. Maybe Linc had changed as much as all that. Maybe there isn't anything more than what the police say. But I can't help feeling that there is something missing in all this, something that hasn't come out yet."

"If I were you," Frank said, leaning across to give Dennis' knee a paternal pat, "I'd leave all that up to the police. It's their job, after all, and you might only make things more complicated for them if you start looking for problems on your own."

"I guess you're probably right, but I would still like to know about this Jeff person. If I could only track him down, find out who he is."

"Maybe he's just a cousin," Frank said. "Or a stock broker Linc called for advice, or the mechanic who works on his car. He could be anybody, don't you see? What makes you think he's in any way involved with Linc's death?"

"I don't know, Dennis admitted. "It's just a feeling I have." He shrugged and finished his drink. "I guess you're right. I shouldn't interfere. I'm lucky to get off without any scandal as it is. I'm grateful to this Mathews for that."

"We're all lucky," Frank agreed, finishing his own drink as well. "This could have been very ugly for all of Linc's friends." He paused. "You know, of course, that Linc kept diaries?"

Dennis was surprised once again. He had known about Linc's diaries himself, but Linc had always referred to them as his "secret papers," and he never showed them to anyone, or even mentioned them. He wondered how Frank had known of their existence.

As though reading his thoughts, Frank chuckled again. "The police questioned me, too, you understand," he said in the way of explanation. "They questioned all of Linc's friends, from what I gather. The diaries came up in the course of their questions. We were all of us in them. It was a little embarrassing."

Dennis smiled in return. "Sorry, I wasn't trying to accuse you of anything. I guess I'm just having trouble facing the facts."

Frank got up to go. "Don't get up," he insisted, coming toward the chair in which Dennis was seated. He dropped a friendly hand on Dennis' shoulder. "I want you to know, if I can do anything to help, feel free to call on me. Maybe when you're feeling a little better, we can get together for a drink or something."

Dennis looked up at the man who had been Linc's friend for so many years. Frank was tall and big, a hulking brute of a man who looked like anything but a homosexual. At the moment, his face was open and friendly, his sympathy obvious.

"Sure, Frank," he said with sincerity, "I'd like that. I could use a friend or two myself right now."

Frank gave his shoulder a squeeze. "Give me a call over the weekend, why don't you?" he suggested. He gave a mock salute and a final smile, and left the apartment.

It wasn't until after he had gone that Dennis remembered that Frank had come for a pair of cuff links, and he had left without ever getting them.

Making his way back into the kitchen, Dennis made a mental note to remind Frank of them when they talked over the weekend.

CHAPTER THREE
◊

Dennis woke in the morning after a bad night's sleep. His mother called soon after he had showered and shaved, to tell him she had made a plane reservation to return east later in the morning.

They had a desultory breakfast together at her hotel, where she asked about his own plans to leave.

"I'm not really sure," he answered, barely picking at his food. He knew that he probably should leave the city now, as soon as possible. The longer he remained here, the longer he stayed at Linc's apartment, the longer the ghost of Linc would continue to haunt him. Yet somehow the urge to remain was too strong to be set aside. He felt compelled to linger, for some reason that he himself could not quite define.

"Well, of course, your vacation has been spoiled for you," his mother said, "But I suppose you might as well be here where it's nice, rather than back in all that nasty weather at home. I'd stay myself, but I'm with the music association now, you know, and there's so much to be done when I get back."

She accepted his decision to stay on without any argument, pursuing instead the subject of her responsibilities with the music association. Dennis was relieved that he did not have to justify his decision to stay. He wasn't sure how he could explain it to someone else. He didn't think he could explain it to himself.

It was nearly noon when he left her at the airport, after seeing her aboard a jetliner. He drove back into the city and, on an impulse, turned away from Linc's apartment and drove instead into the downtown district of Beverly Hills, parking the car outside the police station.

He was in luck: Sergeant Mathews was in. The policeman greeted with him a kindly enough smile and evident curiosity.

"What brings you by?" he asked when they were inside his office. "Did you remember anything important?"

"No, not really," Dennis said, uncertain himself just why he was here. "I wanted to tell you, that grocery list wasn't a clue after all. It belonged to a friend of Linc's, Frank Davenport. He left it there some weeks ago."

Mathews shrugged. "I hadn't really attached too much importance to it anyway. I was more interested in the name of Jeff. Any further thoughts on him?"

"Sorry, I can't tell you any more than I did before. I suppose you checked out all of Linc's... Mister Gardner's friends?"

"Pretty much so," Mathews said. "I didn't expect to find anything in that direction, but it's a routine step. Anyone in particular you're wondering about?" Dennis waited too long before answering.

"Davenport?" Mathews suggested. Dennis' blush confirmed the guess. "Not a chance. While your friend Gardner was entertaining his guest at the piano, Davenport was at a bar in Hollywood, where he talked with several people he knew. What makes you suspicious of him, anyway?"

Dennis smiled sheepishly. "Oh, I didn't actually mean to suggest that I was. It's nothing, really—only, when I knew him in the past, he wasn't very friendly toward me, and now he is."

Mathews looked at him for a long moment. "He might have his reasons," he said. "You're a good looking young man. When he knew you before, you were sort of attached to a friend of his, weren't you? It wouldn't have been exactly tactful of him to show that he was attracted to you."

Dennis blushed again and could think of nothing to say in answer to that blunt assessment of the situation. Oddly, it had never occurred to him that Frank might have been attracted to him in the past. Certainly he had never done anything to show that he was; but as Mathews pointed out, that would have been tactless, considering the relationships between the three of them.

"If I were you," Mathews said, standing, "I wouldn't get myself involved. Why don't you catch the next plane back east, try to forget any of this ever happened."

"I don't think I could forget," Dennis told him, standing also. He started toward the door, but paused and turned back. "Just out of curiosity," he said, "That Hollywood bar you said Mister Davenport was seen in, do you happen to remember the name of the place?"

"Sure," Mathews said, his face expressionless, "The Ship's Call."

* * * * * * *

The phone was ringing when Dennis let himself into the apartment. He answered and found himself talking to Frank.

"I was a little worried about you, all alone in that apartment, with all those memories," Frank said. "So, I picked up a couple of tickets to a piano recital tonight at the Wilshire Ebell. Can I persuade you to go with me tonight?"

Dennis hesitated. He did not really feel in the mood for going out, but at the same time, he felt guilty. He had been a little unfair in his suspicions of Frank. Mathews' insinuation stuck in his mind. Was Frank interested in him? It wasn't entirely unlikely, after all. He and Linc had shared many interests in common. Their tastes weren't terribly different in most matters. He had no idea what Frank's tastes were in men. He had never even thought of that, had no interest in the subject.

Maybe too, he thought, Frank was lonely for Linc. In the past, Linc had been, in a sense, a wall that separated the two of them. Oddly, now, he was more of a tie between them.

"I'd love to go," he decided impetuously. "Where do I meet you?"

"I'll pick you up, make it about six thirty," Frank said, sounding pleased, "And we can have an early dinner before the recital, all right?"

* * * * * * *

The evening proved to be a pleasant one after all. Enjoying an excellent dinner in a booth at the long-established Musso and Frank's restaurant (no relation, Frank had quipped as they came in) in Hollywood, Dennis found himself in much better spirits than he would have expected. Frank had been perfectly right: he did need to get out of the apartment and seek some diversion. He was allowing himself to become morbid, thinking constantly of Linc, and of Linc's death.

It was ironic that Frank should have suggested a piano recital. It was Linc who had awakened Dennis' innate appreciation for the arts, particularly for classical music. At one time, Linc had played the piano, had been well on his way to a successful musical career. There had been an accident, Dennis knew that much, although that was one subject Linc had always refused to discuss with him. His love for music, however, especially for piano music, and his knowledge, had remained with him and he had been an excellent tutor for his younger friend.

Now, it almost seemed as if Frank were stepping in to fill that role in Dennis' life. Dennis refused to consider what other roles Frank might wish to fill, however. Linc had been his first such relationship—he still balked at using the word, "lover"—and so far as he was concerned at the present, probably the last.

"What did happen to Linc?" Dennis asked aloud over dinner, following his own train of thought. "I mean, the accident that interrupted his piano career?"

"It wasn't very pleasant," Frank told him from across the table, pausing to take a sip of his wine. "He was very promising, you know. It looked like he would have a major career. Then, one night, he was playing a recital, at the Loudon conservatory, all Chopin. He played exquisitely, especially Chopin. His music is so difficult. Rubenstein says he should only be played by children and geniuses. Linc was such a genius. I was there that night, standing backstage, and I can tell you, I had tears in my eyes, listening

"He had just finished, and was bowing to the audience. His left hand was on the piano, and suddenly the lid fell, crushing his fingers. He spent a long time in therapy after the hand healed, but he was never able to get the control back, or the strength. Oh, he played, played very nicely for an amateur, but never well enough for a real artist."

Dennis grimaced as he imagined the agony, physical and mental, that the accident must have caused Linc. Yes, he remembered Linc at the piano in the apartment, practicing with his left hand, over and over. To him, of course, it had sounded just fine, but to Linc's own ears the difference must have been painfully obvious.

"You studied with him, didn't you?" he asked.

"Yes, we were friends even then, in the conservatory," Frank said. "Of course, I had to give it up eventually. The family simply couldn't afford the expense. That's when I went into insurance. I suppose in the long run it's just as well. I've done nicely in insurance, I have to say that for myself."

"Was he really that good, Frank?" Dennis wished fervently that he might have heard Linc play; really play, as he must have then, before the accident.

"Yes, but, please, let's not talk ourselves into another black mood. Besides, we have to get moving if we're going to make that recital."

Dennis nodded in agreement. Maybe it was best to leave that subject. If nothing else, he owed it to Frank to make the evening as pleasant as possible, considering the trouble to which Frank had gone for his sake.

The recital was not particularly exciting: a young student giving his first public performance, with nerves evident. Dennis attributed his own lack of enthusiasm in part, too, to the events of the past few days.

In any case, however, it was at least something to occupy their time and their attention, and to get their minds off less pleasant subjects. He felt better on the way home than he had since arriving in California.

"Thanks, I'm glad you suggested this," he told Frank when they were stopped at the curb outside the apartment. "I really mean that, Frank."

Frank switched off the Cadillac's lights. The street was dark and empty, the building set off by itself and surrounded by greenery. To his amazement, Frank turned abruptly and clasped Dennis' hands in his own.

"Dennis," he said softly. He pulled Dennis toward him across the seat.

Dennis was amazed at the man's strength. He offered nothing more than token resistance as Frank embraced him tightly, all but squeezing the breath from his lungs.

"I want you," Frank whispered in his ear. "I've always wanted you...."

His hands made their way passionately over Dennis' body, groping, fondling. Dennis was limp in the powerful arms. He should stop it, now, he told himself, before it went further; but he did not want to hurt Frank, not after the man had been so kind to him. Besides, it had been a long time for him. His body was responding on its own to the touches, swelling and growing rigid.

"No," he gasped, jerking himself free of Frank's embrace.

They sat staring away from one another for a long moment, both of them breathing heavily.

"I'm sorry," Dennis said finally. "Maybe, maybe later, after some time, but not now. I couldn't."

"I understand," Frank said. "God, I'm sorry for that. I promised myself I wouldn't. It won't happen again, I swear it."

Dennis opened the car door and stepped outside. "I had a wonderful time," he said, leaning back into the car. They exchanged strained smiles and Dennis swung the door shut and turned and made his way into the apartment building.

* * * * * * *

Despite that awkward scene with Frank, Dennis slept well for the first time in days. It was nearly noon when he awoke, and he smiled as he remembered how Linc had teased him in the past for sleeping late.

In contrast to his rather good humor, the weather outside had turned gloomy. The sky was gray and the winter rains, which were never mentioned in Chamber of Commerce literature, threatened.

Dennis thought of going out for the day and came close to calling Frank. His appreciation for the previous evening's thoughtfulness had been genuine, and he felt close to Frank in a way he never had before, closer than he had with anyone else other than Linc.

In the end, however, he decided to stay indoors. The rain had finally started falling, a steady downpour. He ate some breakfast alone and decided it would be a good time to go through the things Linc had left behind in the apartment. Perhaps after all there was something that had been overlooked in the police search, the sort of thing that would only be noticed by someone familiar with the place and with Linc's belongings.

He went to the den first, his eyes going at once to the bookshelves that lined one wall. A group of brown leather binders caught his attention. He recognized them at once: the diaries, of course. Although he had known about them, he had never looked into them. They were, after all, Linc's personal property, and he had never shown any inclination to share them.

Now, curious and even a little hopeful that he might gain some new insight into the events that had taken Linc's life, he took one of them from the shelf and opened it. It was dated 1960 on the flyleaf.

He set that one aside and reached for another, at the far end. This one was 1965, the year just ended. Although he checked each of the others in turn, there was none for this year, 1966. Of course, Linc had been murdered on Monday night, the third day of the year. Perhaps he had not gotten around to picking up a new one. Dennis was disappointed; he had hoped he might read something about those three days, maybe even something about Linc's plan for the very evening he had been murdered.

He went back to the one dated 1965—the year he and Linc had been apart. If all that he had heard were true, Linc had changed, changed dramatically, during that year. He had lost interest in waiting for "his Dennis" to come back to him. He had become interested in a different type of companion, had become a patron of a type of bar he had disdained in the past.

Flicking on the light behind the sofa, Dennis turned to the first page of the diary and began to read. It was not an easy task. Even the sight of Linc's handwriting, strangely studied and precise, brought a fresh pang of grief to him. He had read through only two days when he came upon the first mention of his own name.

"...A whole year," he read, "Stretching before me, until I can see my Dennis again. It seems like an eternity; but I can wait, for someone as

46

worthwhile as he is. I know that in time he will come to realize his love for me, and at the end of that year, we will be together again...."

Dennis' eyes clouded with tears and he had to pause to smoke a cigarette, the book turned over on his lap. Reluctantly, he went back to it, determined to read on, to find the answers to the questions that tormented him.

It was not an exciting book, nor scandalous. Mostly it was filled with the trivia of day to day living, or with random thoughts, notations of things to do or things that had been done: a concert attended, with impressions recorded; a reminder to shop for an opera cape his mother wanted.

The winter of the year had become spring, and Linc's social life remained virtually nonexistent, if his record was to be believed. Frank came by for dinner. Linc spent a weekend with his family, at the "funeral parlor." Time and time again he mentioned "my Dennis," miles away, and marked the passing of the months, counting the time that remained of their separation.

With the summer, he had been out more, although usually alone. Once there had been a visitor, a man he had met years before in Paris, who had stopped by for a visit while in this country. Far from being jealous, Dennis was touched by the guilt Linc had suffered as a result of this brief interlude: "What kind of faithless lover am I, that I can't just wait a year for the man I love more than anything in the world?" he asked himself.

With the coming of autumn, his interest in music had come to the fore again. He was composing and was especially enthusiastic over a song, which he intended to dedicate to Dennis.

"...Dennis, I can only imagine what the year has been for him thus far, but I am certain he will come, he will realize that it is right for us...."

Dennis forced himself to read on despite the pain that grew in his chest, smoking one cigarette after another. Linc's life had continued to be a quiet one, one of waiting impatiently for the year to end. There was no mention of bars, no mention of new friends, no sexual experiences but that one with the old friend from Paris. Here and there a day had been left blank. Perhaps he had been afraid to record the events of those days. Perhaps these were the times when he was changing his life, and heading it toward its ultimate tragic end; but there was no indication, when the writing resumed, of anything to hint that those days had been in any way different. They might have been only days when he was occupied, or perhaps just not in the mood for writing in a diary.

The recorded year drew toward its ending, and Linc was busier now, preparing for the holidays, working regularly on the music he was composing, shopping. He saw more of his friends, but they were old friends such as Frank, whom he saw regularly, and others whose names were familiar to Dennis.

Christmas was a nice one, and quiet, spent with the family at the Gardner house. "...A pleasant day, but how much more so it would have been had Dennis been with me. I pray it will be our last one apart."

There was little after that day: a brief note that his father was not well; and then, on the last day of the year, one final entry: "At last, the letter I have waited for, have lived for throughout this long and lonely year. Dennis is coming. He will be here on Wednesday. He doesn't say what his decisions are. I'll have to wait until I see him, I guess, to hear them. But he is coming. He wouldn't come so far, I'm sure, to tell me he doesn't love me. If I can only wait without going to pieces!"

That was all. The year had ended, and so had Linc's life. There was no Jeff in this book, no Ship's Call, no brutal young man in leather. Or, were they there, on the empty pages?

It was still raining outside. Coming back into the living room, Dennis stood at the French doors that opened onto the little balcony, staring through the misted glass at the park beyond.

The questions were still there, still unanswered. Linc had left behind no clues, no message; only a record of his love, and his anxiety.

Dennis leaned his face against the coolness of the rain-streaked glass. He had to know. He had to find out the truth for himself, discover if Mathews was right, or if there were more, which no one suspected; and there was only one way for him to find out.

It was Sunday. The bars here were open on Sundays, and the clues to the mystery of Linc's death were in that bar: The Ship's Call. If he were going to find the truth, he was convinced he would find it there.

He turned away from the window, back to the room. Tonight he would go to The Ship's Call, as

Linc had done. He would find Jeff, whoever he was, and he would learn the answer to the questions that haunted him.

CHAPTER FOUR
◊

Dennis waited until evening before starting out for The Ship's Call. He had dressed in a manner that he hoped would be appropriate for the place, or as appropriate as anything in his wardrobe: jeans, a battered jacket he had found in Linc's closet, loafers, no jewelry. At the door, he picked up Linc's keys where he had left them atop the chest, but once in the garage he changed his mind about driving the Mercedes. It would probably be pretty showy for the type of bar he was expecting, and he did not want to attract a great deal of attention to himself. He dropped Linc's keys into the jacket of the pocket and went instead in the plain Ford he had rented.

The Ship's Call was in Hollywood, in a less than savory neighborhood, flanked on one side by an old bookstore, dark now, and on the other by a shadowy alley. Dennis parked a few blocks away and walked to the bar. At the door, closed against prying eyes, he paused for a moment. He had never been in one of these places, not in any gay bar, in fact, and he had no idea what to expect. Summoning his determination, he pushed open the door and walked inside.

For a moment he could see absolutely nothing in the dim glow of the interior. He stood just inside the door, blinking his eyes, and gradually the room came into view. A semicircle of a bar jutted out into the long, narrow room, and along the opposite wall was a railing and a narrow shelf. Both areas were lined with men, most of them in leather jackets and boots. One wall was decorated with a length of chain and a whip, and near where Dennis stood was a huge poster advertising some motorcycle event.

Several of the bar's customers had turned to stare at Dennis while he stood waiting for his eyes to adjust to the light. Some of the stares were curious, and others frankly interested. Trying to appear at ease in the unfamiliar atmosphere, Dennis walked to the bar and ordered a beer from the man behind it.

He swallowed a quick mouthful of beer, annoyed to notice that he spilled a little of it in his nervousness. To his relief, however, the others in the room had apparently accepted him as "safe," and were no longer staring in his direction. He took advantage of the opportunity to study some of them.

They were a rough looking group, sullen and mostly unfriendly, and not at all the sort of crowd he would have expected to find in a "gay" bar. Again, he was struck by the improbability of Linc's being interested in any of the men who were here. Was Jeff among them, he wondered, one of those rough-edged young men standing around? Dennis could see no one whom he regarded as particularly attractive, although he could see that one or two of them had a brute, wild animal type of appeal.

"You're a new face around here, aren't you?"

The voice at his elbow startled him. Dennis turned in the direction of the wall to see an elderly man seated at the end stool. He looked a bit out of place among all these macho types, although he seemed entirely at ease, and not a little drunk.

"I just moved into town," Dennis said. "Are you a regular?"

The old man giggled in a high-pitched, effeminate voice. "Oh, dear me, yes, I practically live in this place," he said with a simper. "You picked the right spot to start your social life, you know. All these studs, there's always something going on here."

Dennis took another sip of his beer and leaned hopefully closer. "Anything exciting?" he asked.

The eyelashes flicked over bloodshot eyes. "Well, now, that depends on what you call exciting, doll," he answered. "This place got mixed up in a murder not a week ago, but of course you wouldn't have read much about it in the newspapers, nothing about this place, anyway. They always hush those things up when a queer is involved."

Dennis suppressed a burst of excitement. He had to be talking about Linc's murder. "A murder?" he asked dubiously, trying not to reveal the extent of his interest. "Here, in the bar?"

"No, not here, but they met here." The old man was flattered by the attention from this handsome young stranger, and was growing rapidly more enthusiastic in his conversation, clinging drunkenly to the edge of the bar. "At least, that's what the police think."

"You mean that's not the real story?" Dennis asked.

One eye winked coquettishly at him. "Fa de da, you don't think anyone here is going to tell the police the straight of it, do you? Let them think what they want to think, that's how I feel about the police."

Dennis moved impatiently closer, eager to hear more and yet not wanting to frighten his informant. "Oh, I've heard all that before," he said scornfully. "It's the same with every murder in the papers, everyone likes to think they know the inside story about what happened."

The withered face lifted from its contemplation of the bar top. "Oh, you don't need to think I'm handing you a line," he said in a petulant voice. "I'm telling you, it was that Gardner fellow who got murdered, maybe you heard about it. Well, the papers don't say it, but he was in here that very night, I recognized him the minute I saw his picture in the paper, and then the first thing you know, the police are all over this place, asking everybody questions and snooping around—as though they'd get anything out of anyone here. They'd never even have known he had been here if some blabbermouth hadn't tipped them off. I just wish I knew who it was who opened his big mouth about it, is all."

"Yes, but...." Dennis started to pursue the matter, when they were interrupted by a voice from behind him.

"Looks like you've had a few too many, Chuck," someone said.

Dennis had been so absorbed in their conversation, he had been unaware that anyone had approached them. He turned to find himself facing a tall, ruggedly handsome young man, not much older than himself. Like the others in the bar, he wore the leather jacket and boots appropriate to the place, but, unlike some of the others, there was nothing incongruous or affected about his appearance or his manner. He gave the impression of a savage young tiger, fierce and at the same time irresistibly beautiful.

The eyes, a piercing steel blue, were glimmering with a cold light as they stared at and through him. The too-red lips were drawn in a firm line. He could be dangerous, Dennis found himself thinking, instinctively shrinking away from this stranger, the sort of creature, he felt sure, who would let nothing stand in the way of what he wanted.

If the stranger had a disquieting impression on Dennis, he had plainly struck fear in the old man, Chuck. The drunk huddled further back into his corner, looking like a trapped animal.

"We was just having a friendly chat," he whined, "Just me and this young man here."

"As long as you're in the mood for conversation," the stranger addressed him in clipped tone, his back to Dennis, "How about having a little chat with me, okay?"

"Sure, sure, doll," the old man agreed hurriedly. He half fell as he tried to scramble from the stool, and to Dennis' surprise, the stranger grabbed his harm, supporting him as he steered him toward the opposite wall, into an empty corner.

Dennis bit his lip in anger and frustration, and forced himself not to stare after them. He had been on the verge of learning something new, he was sure of it; and he was just as sure that the stranger had known the subject of the conversation too, and that he had interrupted it to prevent old Chuck from saying anything more.

He strained his ears, but it was impossible over the noise of the bar to make out anything more than the sound of their voices, the stranger's low and ominous, Chuck's rising from time to time in a frightened whimper.

"Another beer?" the bartender had approached, watching him with a bored smile.

"Sure, why not," Dennis answered, finishing off what was left in his bottle. He took some change from his pocket, as the fresh beer was set in front of him.

"But, I tell you, Jeff..." It was only a fragment of their argument, carrying over the sounds of the bar, but there was no mistaking the name the old man had spoken.

The coins in Dennis' hand jingled and clattered as they fell to the floor. He shuddered and met the curious eyes of the bartender.

"Guess I'm a little clumsy tonight," he mumbled, stooping to gather up the money from the sawdust littered floor.

"You aren't drunk, are you?" the bartender asked of him as he took the change. "I'm not supposed to serve you if you're already drunk."

"No," Dennis reassured him with his most innocent smile. "No, but I might decide to get that way before the evening is over."

"Well, find somebody to go home with and do it on their time," the man said. "We don't need any trouble here."

Dennis could not help smiling as the bartender drifted away. He was on the right track, he was positive of that. The handsome young stranger in the corner with Chuck was Jeff, and there was no doubt in his mind that he was the right Jeff, the one for whom he was searching. It hadn't been a coincidence that he had interrupted just as old Chuck was talking to him about Linc's murder.

It was impossible to know what lay ahead, what he might uncover. Mathews might even have been right in his theory. Glancing once more in Jeff's direction, Dennis thought that it was not hard to imagine Linc, or anyone else, for that matter, being attracted to this youthful savage. It would be hard to consider the risks of courting such a specimen of rugged manhood.

Whatever the truth was, however, Dennis had to uncover it for himself. Whatever he learned about Linc was better than remaining puzzled and haunted by the questions surrounding his death.

He swore, as he leaned against the bar and waited for the argument in the corner to end, that he had to meet Jeff, had to become better acquainted with him, at any risk.

* * * * * * *

Whatever that argument involved, it seemed to be winding down. Glancing in the direction of the pair, Dennis had the impression that the tension had slackened. Chuck, the old man, was still nervous and rather frightened, but he was smiling and giggling now as he talked.

The discussion ended finally. Chuck, ignoring the beer he had left on the counter, hurried from the bar and disappeared into the night. Dennis breathed deeply, praying that Jeff would not be leaving also. Somehow he had to meet this young Adonis and become acquainted with him.

Jeff himself solved the problem for him. He returned to the corner of the bar that Chuck had deserted and ordered a beer. When it came, he turned toward Dennis and flashed a totally disarming smile.

"Sorry to interrupt you and Chuck," he apologized, "But I had to talk to him about something personal."

So personal, Dennis thought, that the old man had fled the bar like a frightened rabbit. "Oh, that's all right," he said aloud, returning the smile. "To tell you the truth, I don't even remember what we were talking about. Just making conversation, I guess."

The answer seemed to satisfy the newcomer's curiosity. He smiled again, the dark lips parting to reveal gleaming white teeth.

"If I'd really been smart, though" he said, "I'd have asked him to hang around long enough to introduce the two of us."

Dennis blushed and glanced down at the bar top, his smile a combination of triumph and genuine embarrassment. This was his first experience with this sort of thing—cruising, wasn't that what they called it?

"To tell the truth," he said, looking back at the smiling face, "I never got around to introducing myself to Chuck, either. I'm Dennis Eastman."

He held out a hand that was quickly clasped in a rock hard grip. "I'm Sandy," the stranger said.

The friendly expression that Dennis kept glued to his face belied the thoughts racing through his mind. No, he was positive of the name he had overheard. The stranger was lying to him now, and there was only one logical reason for that. He was more than ever convinced that he had found the Jeff for whom he was searching, regardless of the fact that he called himself Sandy.

"I don't think I've seen you around before," Sandy continued. It was obvious that he was interested in getting better acquainted.

"Just moved here from back east," Dennis told him. "A fellow I met told me about this place, and I decided I might as well start checking things out."

"I'm glad you did." There was no doubt regarding the expression in Sandy's eyes. Greenhorn that he was, Dennis knew desire when he saw it. He experienced a moment of fear. What was he going to do once he allowed Sandy to pick him up? Once he had committed himself, he was sure there would be no backing out. Sandy didn't look like the sort to go along with any changing "whims." He looked like a man who meant business, and expected cooperation.

Dennis wondered if he would be able to perform sexually if it came to that. He had only been with one man so far in his entire life. Could he go through the sexual act as a partner of the same person who might have murdered Linc? Or was he perhaps even receiving the same sort of come-on that Linc had received? Was Sandy leading him on, planning to rob and perhaps murder him?

It occurred to him that if Sandy thought he had no money, that would soon answer that question. Dennis finished the last of his beer.

"I guess that's it for the night," he announced. "I've really got to pinch the pennies until I find myself a job."

Sandy said nothing in reply. Dennis buttoned up his jacket slowly, wondering if he had gambled too soon. Maybe Sandy wasn't yet interested enough to pick him up, and now he had committed himself to leaving. Discouraged, and still moving slowly, he turned toward the door.

"Can I give you a lift?" Sandy asked abruptly.

Dennis stopped with a smile of relief. "Swell," he agreed quickly. He could always come back for the car some other time. This was an opportunity he couldn't afford to pass up.

Sandy polished off his own beer and took a cap off a peg on the wall nearby. Outside, he led the way to the alley at one side of the bar and started down it. Dennis followed him with some reluctance and a return of his fear. It was possible that Sandy had guessed the truth after all, that trouble might come down this darkened alley; but it was too late now to back out.

"Got time to come by my place for another beer?" Sandy asked, turning to glance at him.

Again, Dennis smiled with real relief. "Sure, I'd love one," he declared. At least he knew Sandy's

GOODBYE, MY LOVER, BY VICTOR J. BANIS

interest in him was genuine. "If you're sure you
don't mind."

Sandy laughed, a surprisingly friendly sound,
warm and natural, and very masculine. "You
know," he said, "I'm beginning to wonder if you
aren't a virgin. Don't you even know when you've
been picked up?"

Dennis laughed too, a trifle more nervously.
"To tell you the truth, I am totally new at all this,"
he said, "But I am willing to learn."

Sandy stopped, his expression serious. "Are
you sure you want to?"

Dennis met the intense gaze evenly. "I'm
sure," he insisted.

They started off again, and rounded the back
corner of the building, and came into a small, as-
phalt parking area. There were three or four motor-
cycles parked there. Sandy went to one of them and
took the key from his pocket. His cap was under his
arm and he handed that to Dennis.

"Here, hold this," he said.

His thoughts preoccupied with what might lie
ahead, Dennis clumsily dropped the cap.

"Hey, you are nervous, aren't you?" Sandy
said, studying him intently again. "Are you sure you
don't want to change your mind? No hard feelings. I
know how scary it can be when you're just coming
out."

Dennis shook his head. "No, I'm sure," he
said, trying to think of some logical explanation for
his nervousness. His companion was obviously no
fool, much sharper than he would have expected.

"It's the bike," he said with an embarrassed grin. "I've never ridden one of these things. I've always been a little nervous about them."

It was far from the truth. In high school a close friend had owned a motorcycle and he had ridden on it and even driven it himself on many occasions; but the lie worked.

"Is that all?" Sandy dropped a friendly arm around his shoulder. "Well, don't get yourself in a lather about that. I only live a few blocks from here, we can leave the bike and walk, okay?"

"Aren't you afraid someone will steal it?"

"Here? No, I've left it here before. There's no one around here at this time of night but the guys at the bar, and they all love bikes too well to tamper with someone else's."

"I guess the walk would do me good," Dennis said with a grateful nod.

They left the alley and went back to the street, and started off walking in the direction Sandy indicated. Neither of them spoke much, although Sandy seemed perfectly at ease. If he were suspicious, he gave no indication of it.

The street they were on took them over the freeway. Beneath their feet, heavy streams of traffic dashed in either direction, their headlights forming ribbons of light—the quintessential Los Angeles, the city of automobiles.

"Cigarette?" Sandy asked, extending the pack.

"Thanks," Dennis answered, accepting one. They paused. Sandy cupped his hands and struck a match, and they moved close together to shield the match from the night wind. As the light flared, Dennis studied the chiseled features of the face close to his own. Was this the right one? Was he really on the right track? He had no desire to go through with what might turn out to be a very unpleasant evening, only to discover that he had been mistaken.

"Thanks, Jeff," he said, inhaling from the cigarette.

The hand with the match paused in mid-air, the steel blue eyes widened and turned suddenly cold. All of the friendly companionship that Sandy had shown before was gone in one instant.

Instinctively, Dennis leaned backward, away from the stony face and those hard eyes peering at him. His back touched the railing behind him and he thought dizzily of the freeway below and those racing cars. It would take only one violent shove, one off-balance moment, and he would topple over the railing, would fall onto the freeway, into the path of those cars....

"Sorry," he said quickly, with a little laugh that he hoped sounded more embarrassed than fearful. "It's Sandy, of course, I do know that. You remind me of someone I knew. His name was Jeff. You look a lot like him. I was just thinking of him, is all."

The steely eyes continued to regard him coldly for a moment. Then, abruptly, Sandy tossed the match over the railing and looked away. They resumed their walk in silence.

"So, who was this Jeff you knew?" Sandy asked after a few minute.

"Just a friend," Dennis said. "A very close friend. To be honest, that's why I've been so nervous. Like I said, you remind me a lot of him. Being with you, here, like this, it's made me think of him. I've kind of had him on my mind since I first saw you."

"A lover?" Sandy asked, glancing sideways.

Relieved for the explanation, Dennis nodded. "Sort of, I guess," he said, "Although we never really got around to calling it that."

"What happened to him?"

"He...he died."

The statement seemed to soften Sandy's attitude. "I'm sorry," he said. He gave Dennis' arm a firm squeeze. "That must have been pretty unpleasant for you. Your first one and all."

The tension relaxed after that and they walked on once again in the more comfortable mood they had shared before. Dennis' thoughts continued to clash with one another. He had taken a chance on using the name, a dangerous chance; and "Sandy" had reacted to it strongly. But his reaction might merely have been annoyance at having his name forgotten. If he had really been afraid, if he were really Jeff and a murderer, the opportunity had been there for him to eliminate an obvious threat. If he were guilty, would he have accepted the explanation so readily? Or was he perhaps biding his time, waiting until they reached the apartment, where there was less danger of a witness?

Despite the nonchalance that he assumed, Dennis was all too aware of the fact that he was walking with danger, perhaps moving toward the same fate that had been Linc's. He was prepared, of course, to put up a fight, but a gun could make any fight uneven, and Linc had been shot. Linc himself had been no pantywaist, but his well-muscled and cared-for body had not kept him alive.

GOODBYE, MY LOVER, BY VICTOR J. BANIS

CHAPTER FIVE
◊

The building in which Sandy lived was an older one, apparently a house that had been divided at some time in the past into apartments. That was something to be grateful for, Dennis decided as he followed his companion inside. Surely there were other people in the building, people who would hear a gunshot and summon the police. Even if he lost his life, he would be leading the police to the man they were seeking.

"This isn't exactly a palace, I'm afraid," Sandy said, opening the door into the apartment. "But it's comfortable and it's cheap."

He flicked on a light and took off his leather jacket. Dennis gave him his jacket as well and Sandy took them to a closet at one end of the room to hang them up.

Dennis followed him into the room, pausing beside a table that stood at one wall. There was mail lying on the table, several envelopes. He glanced in Sandy's direction, but Sandy's back was to him. With a quick movement, Dennis flipped one of the letters over. It was addressed to a Mister Jeff Conrad! Triumphantly, he moved away from the table. There had been no mistake, then, he was with the right person, the man he had wanted to find. And Sandy had lied about his name.

"Still want that beer?" Sandy asked, turning from the closet and coming across the room to pause just in front of Dennis. The form fitting t-shirt he wore under the jacket revealed his body more fully than had been the case before. Beneath the wide shoulders his arms bulged with rocklike muscles, not the pumped up muscles of the body builder, but the arms of a powerful and athletic man. His solid chest tapered to a narrow waist and below that, skin tight pants clung to slender hips, revealing in the front still more evidence of his ample manhood. It was a body that reeked of sex and masculine beauty. Inexperienced as he was, Dennis found himself uncomfortably aware of its nearness. He swallowed hard.

"I guess so," he answered, trying not to stare at the man before him. Now that he was here, he was not at all sure what he should do next. He could hardly ask Sandy bluntly for the truth. He would have to advance slowly, first gain the other's confidence. Take your time, he warned himself silently.

"You do know, don't you," Sandy said, coming still closer, "That wasn't the only reason I invited you up here? It wasn't even the most important one."

That statement could mean any number of things, Dennis found himself thinking; but the gleam in Sandy's eyes was easy to recognize.

"I know," he answered with a smile. He did not have to fake the warmth of the smile. Never before had he felt so keenly the attraction for another male's body. With Linc, it had been different, it had grown out of their friendship; but he could not deny the fact that the man before him was overwhelmingly appealing, despite any nervousness or fear that he might feel.

Sandy reached for him, his strong hands clasping Dennis' waist firmly, and drawing him close. Dennis felt his own body pressed tightly against the hardness of the other, as the commanding arms encircled him in an embrace. Sandy was taller than he was by several inches and, without thinking Dennis lifted his face, his eyes closed. He felt the warmth of the deep red lips upon his own.

He had never been kissed the way Sandy kissed him. Linc was the only other man who had ever kissed him, but even that had not been the same. This was wild and animal, exciting beyond description. Whatever lingering doubts he might have had about his attraction to men disappeared in the fervent heat of that kiss.

"The bedroom's in there," Sandy whispered hoarsely in his ear.

They separated and Dennis moved in the direction of the nod, into the bedroom. He glanced back once and his heart stopped. Sandy had gone back to turn off the light, and he had stopped at the table that held the letters, staring down at the one that had been turned over.

Dennis went on into the bedroom, fearful again. It was too late now, though, to retreat. He had to go on with the game he had started, praying that

Sandy had not guessed the truth. And, even if it were possible, he wondered if he would be able to back out now. He was dazed by the raging desire that he felt for Sandy, a sheer physical lust that he had never known before.

Nervously aware that anything might be in store for him, he began hurriedly to undress. He heard Sandy go into the bathroom and he glanced around the bedroom, wishing that he could take time to look around, but he didn't dare arouse Sandy's suspicions any further. Perhaps there would be time later, when he had won Sandy's confidence, to search the apartment. For now, it was best to concentrate on the situation at hand.

He slid his boxer shorts down over his hips and tossed them into the chair where he had placed his other clothes. Naked, he was an epitome of youthful, masculine beauty, far more so than he himself had ever realized. His body was slender, the muscles rippling beneath the tight smoothness of his skin. The golden skin was free of hair except for that under his arms, until it reached his lower body. The molded buttocks, softly round and yet firm, were given an enticing luster by the golden hair, little more than down, that lined them, and in the front, a thin trail of the same down started at his navel, running across the flat, hard abdomen to burst into a sea of golden silk, and below his swelling organ and downy orbs, trailed over his firmly muscled legs.

There was a low whistle of appreciation behind him, and Dennis turned to see Sandy in the bathroom doorway, his eyes feasting on the naked beauty before him. With a nervous smile and a blush, Dennis went to the bed, reclining on its surface.

He watched with mounting eagerness as Sandy quickly undressed, baring his tall, powerful body. The same dark hair that lay in wayward curls over his forehead curled on his massive chest as well, and sprang again from the hollow of his navel to cascade downward, carrying the eye to the prize hanging there. Dennis could only stare in awe at his companion's masculine endowments. He was accustomed to seeing naked men, during his athletic activities in school and later in his military service, but Sandy surpassed anything he had seen before, and for the first time Dennis could appreciate the term, "stud." This was a veritable bull of a man, built to inspire desire, and even fear, in those who looked upon his nakedness.

Sandy crossed to the light switch by the door. He paused once to look back at the bed where Dennis waited for him, and his face was filled with the same naked lust that Dennis felt. The switch clicked and the room was plunged into darkness, alleviated only by the faint light that filtered through the curtained window.

The bed creaked slightly as Sandy joined him and searching hands reached for him again. Dennis was tense now with fear, of more than one kind, unsure of himself, or what he should do, how he should act. This was all so different from anything he had yet experienced. Strong arms pulled him close and Sandy's mouth sought his hungrily.

The touch of their bodies as they came together was like an electric shock, jolting Dennis from his fear. He surrendered finally and totally to the desire burning within him, clinging in frantic passion to his partner. Sandy's hands were upon him, grasping, searching, roughly fondling. Dennis felt his flesh come alive in the demanding grip, swelling to its rigid and trembling utmost.

"Don't be afraid," Sandy whispered in the darkness. "I'll be gentle." His mouth began to burn a trail over Dennis' quivering body, his tongue a searing flame that made its way downward over his throat, his chest, his abdomen, seeking, hungrily demanding.

Dennis moaned aloud with agonized pleasure. It had been so long, so long, and the touch of those lips upon his flesh had shattered the gates of his reluctance, releasing a flood of passion that swept through and over him. The brush of Sandy's hair against his thighs was like a thousand fingers urging him onward, upward.

He felt his legs lifted into the air and rested on broad, powerful shoulders, and for a moment Dennis' fear returned. He had never done this before, not even with Linc. He thought of Sandy's body as it had been revealed a moment before, of the mammoth proportions he had seen and that he now felt pressed against him; but it was too late to protest. Sandy did not wait for permission, and Dennis was too consumed now with flaming lust to resist.

Sandy leaned away from him for a moment. Dennis heard a drawer open and, a minute later, close, and he saw vaguely that Sandy was smearing something on himself. Then, again, he leaned closer.

Dennis felt a sharp stab of pain and flung his hand over his mouth to keep from crying out. Above him, Sandy's wide back was arched, his muscles straining. Dennis' pain increased as a scorching column of flame inching its way inside of him. He raised his buttocks from the bed, trying to ease the effort, biting into the back of his hand savagely.

Sandy lunged at him again, a brutal move, and it was done, possession complete. He paused like that for a moment. "It's easier if you do it all at once," he whispered, bending down to kiss Dennis' mouth. "It'll be better now."

Surprisingly, Dennis found that it was. The pain remained, but it was no longer an agony, and now it carried with it as well a delirious sense of pleasure that he had not imagined could happen to him. Each thrust of the body above him only fanned the flames of his ardor all the more, and Dennis found himself responding, arching his back to help, actually welcoming the massive invader into him. He writhed and twisted as Sandy's mouth again found him. The room seemed to reel and shake as they raced wildly on to their fulfillment.

Dennis grew rigid as the moment neared, his body arched high into the air, and he clutched frantically at Sandy's head. The room exploded into a million shattering lights and he gave himself up to a maddened finale. Sandy's hands clutched at him and he crashed forward, driving himself to the utmost, and joined Dennis in his ecstasy.

Limp and exhausted, Dennis fell back against the pillows. No, he thought, he could not blame Linc for courting any danger, not for the sake of this sort of satisfaction. Whatever danger he himself might face, he knew that he would risk it over and over to have this savage animal again, and again.

* * * * * * *

For a few moments Dennis lay half asleep, half awake, not thinking, merely enjoying the sensation of lazy contentment. The scent of fresh coffee filled his nostrils, luring him into consciousness. He opened one eye and then the other, glancing to the left and then the right. The room was unfamiliar and for a moment he was puzzled by his surroundings.

Memory came back to him then, bringing a smile to his face as he remembered the night he had spent here in this room, in this bed. He thought of the vital, magnificent young body that time and time again through the night had sought his, remembered the summits of ecstasy to which he had soared over and over again. As a lover, Sandy had been inexhaustible, and to his astonishment, he had matched Sandy's ardor stroke for stroke, climax for climax, as he had never done with anyone before, not even with Linc.

The smile faded. Yes, it had been a night such as he had never known or even dreamed of; and Sandy, the man who had given him all that pleasure, was the man he suspected of murdering Linc.

Was it possible? There was a savagery and a ferocity about Sandy, even in his lovemaking, that made anything conceivable. In the right circumstances, there was perhaps no limit to what he might do; and yet the very thought brought a pang of sadness to Dennis. It was hard to believe that the same man who had introduced him to such bliss could also have caused him so much grief.

"Good morning, sleepyhead."

Dennis lifted his head from the pillow and looked toward the door of the room, to see Sandy standing there, smiling at him. He was struck again by the overwhelming beauty of this Greek god, who might very well have descended from Olympus for the pleasure of mere mortals below. In the morning sunlight, stripped of the leather trappings he had worn the night before at the bar, he looked younger and less vicious. He was still splendidly naked, the light playing upon his gleaming flesh as he moved. Incredibly, beneath the sheet Dennis felt his own body stirring with renewed ardor as Sandy crossed the room toward him, his pendulous flesh swinging indolently with each step.

"Do I smell coffee?" Dennis asked, trying to still the pounding in his heart as Sandy bent to kiss him good morning.

"Umm hum," Sandy answered, reaching brazenly beneath the sheet, "But you have to earn it."

Dennis' breath quickened as the sheet was pulled slowly down to reveal his own fully aroused body, rigid and expectant. He sighed with pleasure as Sandy kissed his hard flesh, the darting tongue inspiring a fresh wave of passion. Eagerly he twisted about, reached for the bronzed body kneeling over him, his mouth savoring the sweetness of the swelling flesh that was offered to him. Mouth to body, body to mouth, they clung to one another, discovering anew the delights of their beautiful young bodies. They thrashed and twisted, rolling on the bed, naked flesh slapping against naked flesh. Faster and faster they lunged until Dennis felt that he could endure no more.

They erupted in unison, soaring into a netherworld of throbbing flesh and strangled moans. Clinging weakly to one another, they drifted slowly back to earth, savoring the lingering sweetness of their fulfillment.

"Did I earn the coffee?" Dennis asked after an eternity.

Sandy laughed and slapped his naked bottom soundly. "I think you earned a lot more than coffee," he said, standing. "Oh, no you don't," he said when Dennis reached for his trousers, "I like my meals with a view."

Dennis blushed with lingering modesty, but he tossed the trousers obediently aside and followed Sandy toward the kitchen, both of them resplendently nude. While he sipped the strong, hot coffee that Sandy poured for him, Sandy busied himself at the stove. In a few minutes he set a platter of eggs and bacon on the table.

They attacked the breakfast with relish, setting aside conversation until they had devoured every scrap of the food in front of them.

"I'd say we worked up pretty healthy appetites with all the night's activity," Sandy said, pouring them both fresh coffees.

"At this rate I'll soon be fat," Dennis said, patting his stomach contentedly.

"I know a good way to work it off," Sandy said, getting up to collect the dishes. He leaned down to kiss Dennis briefly.

"Not until I get some rest," Dennis said, pushing him away. "Do you want to kill me?"

He was grateful when he had said it that Sandy had turned his back to him to put the dishes in the sink, and did not see the quick little frown that crossed his face. He had forgotten his reason for being here, for striking up an acquaintance with Sandy. The comment, made in jest, brought it all back to him once again. If Sandy knew all of his motives, he might very well want to kill him.

Despite his concern, however, Dennis could not help smiling. If that was how Sandy meant to do him in, he thought silently, it would certainly be one hell of a way to go.

With the breakfast dishes finished—Sandy washing, Dennis drying—they dressed at last. Dennis hesitated when Sandy offered to drive him home. After his comments the night before about being short of money, the Beverly Hills apartment might be a little hard to explain.

"I can catch a bus," he insisted as they left the apartment together.

"Don't be silly," Sandy said. "I want you to get lots of rest, to get your strength back. Besides, the night I just spent was well worth the gas it will take to drive you home."

"I hope there will be other nights," Dennis said shyly. Now that he had found his suspect, he did not want to lose him again, for more reasons than one.

"I'm glad to hear you say that," Sandy said with a broad grin. "I was afraid you were strictly a one-night-stand type, the way most virgins are. As a matter of fact, what's wrong with tonight for an encore?"

"Not a thing," Dennis said with an answering grin.

To his surprise, instead of starting back to The Ship's Call, where Sandy had left his motorcycle, they headed for the garage in the rear of the building.

"Hey, aren't you forgetting where you left your bike?" Dennis asked. "I know you didn't have any opportunity to go back for it last night, you were too busy riding other things."

Sandy laughed and opened the door to the garage. "No, it's still there. As a matter of fact, it's not even mine. It belongs to my brother. I'll pick it up later."

A battered old MG TD sports car sat in the garage. "It'll be a little cool," Sandy said, indicating the convertible. "There's no top, but I'll put the heater on. It's less uncomfortable than you would think. You sit so low, most of the cold air goes past over your head."

"To be honest," Dennis said, sliding into the passenger's seat, "I'm grateful to have a car to sit in. The way I feel this morning, I don't know if I could hang on to a bike, and I'm sure my backside got plenty enough pounding last night."

Sandy laughed and drove out of the garage and waited while Dennis jumped out to shut the garage door, and climbed back in.

"Which way?" he asked, pulling out into the street.

"I'm staying with a friend," Dennis said, the explanation he had thought of. "Out in Beverly Hills."

Sandy cocked an eyebrow. "Sounds like an okay sort of friend to me."

Dennis laughed. "Don't worry, he's not one of us. Someone I knew from school back east."

The explanation seemed to suffice. Sandy followed his directions without questioning the matter further, and a short time later they pulled up in front of the apartment building. Sandy gave no indication that he recognized it—but, if he had been here before, it was at night, and today they were in broad daylight.

"Sure you don't want me to pick you up tonight?" Sandy asked.

"Thanks, but no, I can get there," Dennis said.

Sandy shrugged. "See you there, then" he said, and drove away.

At the door to the apartment, Dennis reached into the pocket of his jacket and pulled out the ring of keys that had been Linc's. He fitted the house key into the lock and turned the knob, only to find that the door remained stubbornly locked. Puzzled, he examined the keys on the ring again. There were only three of them, and he knew that the other two were for the car.

With a shrug he reached into his other pocket and removed his own key, letting himself in with that. He remembered, as he went inside, that he had left his rented car on the street near The Ship's Call and, with a frown of annoyance, he went back out to find a cab.

* * * * * * *

It was afternoon by the time he made it back to the apartment. The phone was ringing as he came in the front door, and he hurried to answer it.

"Oh, there you are," Frank Davenport's voice greeted him. "I've been calling. I was afraid you had changed your mind and left town after all."

"No, I was with a friend," Dennis said. He wasn't sure that he wanted to let Frank know just where he had been, or why. Anyway, what had happened to him the night before was still too new for him to discuss it with anyone.

"Well, it sounds like you're in better spirits, at least," Frank said.

"Yes, as a matter of fact, I am," Dennis agreed, somewhat to his own surprise. He had not really thought of it, but he was feeling remarkably fine this afternoon. Of course, if sex was a way to relieve tension, he certainly ought to be stress free today, he thought wryly.

Frank waited, as if hoping for more of an explanation. When it didn't come, he said, "I won't keep you, then. But, when I was there the other day, I forgot about some phonograph records I had left, some practice records. Linc wanted to hear them and I left them with him, but of course, now I may as well get them back. Do you mind if I stop by this evening and pick them up?"

"Umm, I'm afraid I'm going out this evening. How about if I bring them over to you tomorrow? I owe you lunch anyway."

Frank paused before answering. "Yes, that will be fine, and lunch sounds good, too. I don't know where you'll find the records, but they won't be hard to recognize. They have no labels on them. Like I said, they're just some practice records. I hired a studio one afternoon and played a few selections, to hear how I sounded these days. Vanity, I'm afraid. I'm also afraid they weren't terribly good. I don't know if Linc ever did listen to them. He didn't' say, but maybe he was being kind. Do me a favor, if you find them, don't listen. It will only embarrass me."

"I'll find them," Dennis assured him. "And I promise I won't listen, although you're probably being too hard on yourself. See you tomorrow, then."

When he had hung up, Dennis went to the record cabinet and looked through the records there without finding any with no labels. He was about to call Frank back when he thought of the phonograph itself. Linc had always had a bad habit of leaving discs on the turntable.

The hunch turned out to be correct. They were on the turntable, three records without labels. He slipped them off the spindle and then, on an impulse, put one of them back and flipped on the machine.

The records were of a poor technical quality, but as Frank had said they were only practice records, the kind used by pianists to study their own mistakes. He smiled as he thought of Frank, who had wanted so badly to be a musician. Linc had told him that, in fact, Frank's lack had been more in talent than in finances.

To Dennis' untrained ear, the playing on the records sounded fine, the touch far more delicate than one would have imagined the burly Frank to possess. A wrong note marred the concerto he was playing, and Frank had started the passage over. Again he had difficulty in the same spot, and again he repeated the passage before going on.

With a pained grin, Dennis flipped the machine off and removed the platter, stacking it with the other two on top of the cabinet, where he would see them and remember to deliver them to Frank the next day.

He stretched wearily and thought of his date later that evening with Sandy. His mind went back to the night before, and he decided with a smug grin that perhaps he had best take advantage of a nap. He hadn't gotten a lot of sleep the night before, and at the rate he and Sandy were going, he would need all the rest he could get.

CHAPTER SIX

◇

Sandy was standing with a group along one wall when Dennis arrived later at The Ship's Call. He saw Dennis come in the door and waved cheerfully, motioning Dennis to join them.

Sandy introduced the three he was with as Jack, Eddie and Mark. Jack said that he had been in the bar the night before, although Dennis did not remember him.

"As a matter of fact," Jack went on with an exaggerated leer, "I was about to move in on you when Sandy took over. I was just complaining about him taking you out of here so quick. He thinks all the really gorgeous ones belong to him."

Dennis was not yet comfortable with the flirtatious manner affected in these places and he blushed and made no answer to the comment.

"If you get tired of this guy," Eddie said, nodding toward Sandy, "Look me up some time. I could teach you some new tricks."

"Come on," Sandy said firmly, leading Dennis toward an empty section of the bar, "Let's get away from these wolves before they try to steal you from me."

At the bar, he ordered beers for both of them and looked Dennis up and down appraisingly. "Yep, you look as good as I remembered," he said.

"You mean you were considering turning me over to your friends there?" Dennis asked.

"Not likely," Sandy assured him. "Anyway, they're a rough crew. I don't think you'd go for them."

"What's so different about them?" Dennis asked, glancing in the direction of the trio.

"Jack and Mark are definitely S&M, the really rough stuff, with chains and all, and Eddie's one of the golden shower boys." He turned to hand Dennis his beer and laughed aloud as he saw the puzzled expression on Dennis' face. "You know," he said, "I don't think you have the vaguest idea what I was talking about."

"I don't," Dennis admitted sheepishly.

"How in the hell did you wind up here without knowing any of that stuff?"

"I told you, a man I met suggested the place," Dennis insisted.

Sandy grew sober again. "S&M, my little friend, stands for sadomasochism. Some of these guys go for it in a big way, burning or beating one another, anything to do with pain. Giving it—that's the sadist—or receiving it, that's the masochist. As for the golden shower, that's something else again."

Dennis thought for a moment, and stared at him dumbfounded. "You don't mean they...?"

Sandy nodded. "They sure do. Like I said, some of these fellows are pretty way out. Believe me, that's mild compared to what some of the guys who come here like."

Dennis looked away and then back at Sandy. "But you come here," he said. "Don't tell me that you...?" He hesitated.

Sandy laughed again. "No, that's not for me, don't worry. You got a pretty good sampling of my tastes in sex last night, there wasn't too much that we missed. I just happen to know a lot of the fellows who come here. Besides, I have a reason for hanging around here just now, a personal reason. Don't worry, though, it has nothing to do with you. I'm not about to swap you for somebody else, and don't think you're going to get rid of me without a fight."

Dennis wondered if that "personal reason" might not have quite a bit to do with him. It was entirely possible that Sandy was watching out for any slip-ups, such as Chuck's the night before.

"You dress like the others," he pointed out.

"The leather? I dress this way when I'm coming here, just so the guys won't feel uncomfortable around me. I have ridden a bike in the past, even raced them a few times, but I never quite got the bug the way some of them do."

Dennis was relieved to learn that Sandy was not like the others he had been describing. He was rapidly discovering that the homosexual underground was far vaster and more complex than anything he had ever imagined.

His relief was tinged with confusion, though. With each new thing he learned about Sandy, his impression of the young man changed. If Sandy was a person of many facets, then it was possible that

Linc might have been engaged in a real affair with him, something more than just a casual pickup. On the other hand, Sandy was appearing to him less and less like a murderer. He was not, after all, one hundred percent animal, although there was certainly a savage and untamed side to his personality.

"Want another?" Sandy asked when they had finished their beers.

"No thanks," Dennis said. "You still owe me one at your apartment, as I recall."

"Always happy to pay my debts," Sandy said with a wink.

* * * * * * *

Back at his apartment, Sandy opened two cans of beer and carried them into the bedroom, setting one on either side of the bed.

"Make yourself at home," he said, and disappeared into the bathroom.

Dennis started to unbutton his shirt, then paused. Sooner or later he was going to have to look around the apartment to see if he could find anything to connect Sandy with Linc. He had already noticed that the letters were gone from the table in the living room. He moved quietly to the dresser, looking over the odds and ends scattered about on its top surface. There was nothing there of any significance. With a pang of guilt, he slid one of the top drawers halfway open.

A leather-encased arm shot suddenly around him, catching him at the throat in an iron grip. He lurched forward, crashing against the dresser as he struggled to free himself from his unknown assailant.

"What the hell?" It was Sandy's voice, coming from the direction of the doorway.

The arm released its hold on his throat and a violent shove that caught him off balance sent Dennis sprawling across the bed. Dazed, he shook his head as he scrambled to his feet, prepared to defend himself against the leather-jacketed stranger who had attacked him.

"Knock it off," Sandy ordered, grabbing the stranger's arm and whirling him about. "What the hell do you think you're doing?"

"I caught him snooping around," the stranger roared angrily. "He was going through the dresser drawers."

Sandy shot a questioning look in Dennis' direction.

"I was looking for a light," Dennis explained breathlessly, nodding his head in the direction of his cigarettes, which had fallen from his pocket to the floor, "When this goon jumped me from out of nowhere."

"You dirty little cocksucker." The stranger started toward him again, but Sandy blocked the way.

"I said, knock it off," he ordered. The stranger came to a halt, although he continued to glower menacingly at Dennis.

"Do me a favor, Dennis," Sandy said without looking at him. "Wait in the other room for a couple of minutes, okay?"

Without saying a word, Dennis went past the two of them and left the bedroom, closing the door after him. He paused in the living room, rubbing his neck gingerly, then turned back toward the bedroom door. The walls of the house, however, were old and thick, and he could hear no more than an unintelligible mumble of voices. If he put his ear to the door…but, no, he decided, it would be a drastic mistake to get caught snooping again. He was just grateful that his matches had been in the pocket of his pants, where they couldn't give a lie to the excuse he had made.

He wondered if Sandy had believed him. Apparently so; if the two of them thought themselves in any danger, they would scarcely have sent him out here where he could make an escape if he wanted.

Which left the all-important question: who was this newcomer? Sandy had not mentioned that he had a roommate, yet the stranger had certainly made himself at home in the apartment. His motorcycle cap was tossed on the sofa, and he must have had a key to let himself in. The door had been locked, and no one had knocked or rung a doorbell.

The voices came nearer to the bedroom door. Not wanting to arouse any further suspicion, Dennis dived for a chair, seating himself in it just as the door opened and the two came into the living room.

The stranger came directly to Dennis, wearing a sheepish expression, his hand extended. "Sorry I lost my head in there," he apologized, shaking Dennis' hand warmly. "Sandy didn't tell me he was seeing anyone these days. I'm his brother, Don."

"It's okay," Dennis assured him. "I guess it must have looked pretty peculiar to you."

"Look, I'm gonna take off," Don went on, picking up his cap from the sofa. "You two won't want me hanging around. Knowing my horny brother, I feel sure you've got things on your minds to do. I'll see you tomorrow, Sandy, okay?"

"Sure, tomorrow," Sandy replied.

Don stopped at the door to look back at Dennis again. "I always did say, my brother knew how to pick 'em," he said, his eyes moving up and down Dennis' body. "Tell you what, if you'd like to try a real man sometime, give me a call, okay? If you think he's big, wait'll you see what I've got."

"Scram," Sandy told him with a jerk of his head. "He's spoken for, for a long time to come."

"Well, maybe that depends on what comes, or who," Don said. He gave Dennis a final, lewd wink before disappearing through the door.

"Sorry about all that," Sandy said, his gaze coming back to Dennis. "I figured you two would meet eventually, but I didn't anticipate anything quite so violent."

Dennis gave him an embarrassed grin. "That'll teach me not to forget my manners," he said. "I could just have waited for you to come back and find me a match."

He breathed easier at Sandy's laugh. There was no indication that Sandy suspected anything awry. He had gotten away with his slip-up…this time. "I'm still waiting for that beer," he said.

"Come on," Sandy said, heading toward the bedroom. "And forget the beer. We're just wasting time out here."

* * * * * * *

Dennis let himself into Linc's apartment the following morning, still puzzling over the events of the previous evening.

Sandy's brother, Don, had been a complete surprise to him. Sandy had never mentioned a brother in their conversations; and although it was not yet clear to him how, he was convinced that somehow Don fitted into the picture as far as Linc's death was concerned. Why else would Sandy, dropping him off this morning, have asked him not to mention meeting Don to anyone?

What was more, notwithstanding the fact that they had enjoyed plenty of red-hot sex again, it was obvious to him that Sandy had been preoccupied since that scene the evening before. Of course, it was entirely possible that Don's accusation had roused Sandy's suspicions after all, but he had certainly remained friendly and affectionate, apart from the sex. It was only that his thoughts had often seemed to be somewhere else.

Dennis was not entirely happy with his own circumstances, either. With each meeting, he found himself growing increasingly fond of Sandy. Yet he remained convinced that Sandy was the Jeff who had been involved in Linc's death, and eventually, whatever he learned would have to be shared with the police, with Sergeant Mathews at least. It was not pleasant to imagine Sandy in prison, shut away from the world, even executed, thanks to his efforts.

He tried to put these troublesome issues aside. He changed his clothes, remembering that he had promised to deliver Frank's phonograph records to him, and buy him lunch. It was actually something of a relief to know that he could be himself for a little while. Playing a role and pretending, constantly on the alert, was proving to be a nerve-racking experience, particularly as he came to like Sandy more and more. He felt like a sneak, lying to him the way he was. More than once he had been tempted to tell him everything, and ask him outright for the truth. Some instinct had prevented him from doing so each time, and the conviction that there was still much he should learn before making any such drastic decisions.

It was far too early to be thinking of lunch. Maybe, he thought, he could persuade Frank to take a rain check on the lunch. Frank lived down near the beach. Taking the records with him, he got Linc's Mercedes out of the garage and headed across town, taking Sunset Boulevard in the direction of Santa Monica.

* * * * * * *

Frank greeted him at the door with an expression of surprise. "Good heavens, I wasn't expecting you so early," he said.

"I thought maybe we could make lunch another day," Dennis said. "I've just got so much on my mind at the moment."

"Of course," Frank said. "But come on in, I'll fix us some coffee at least."

"Thanks, I could us some." Dennis followed him in, setting the records atop the phonograph in the small living room.

"Make yourself at home," Frank told him, going on into the adjoining dining area. "I was just working on some business papers. I'll get them out of the way." While he spoke he was busy gathering up a stack of papers from the dining table, stuffing them into a battered looking briefcase.

"Let me just put these in the bedroom," he said, motioning for Dennis to have a seat at the table. "I'll be right back."

Dennis pulled out a chair, and as he did so, his eyes fell upon a piece of white paper on the floor. One of Frank's business papers, he thought, that had fallen from the table. He stooped to pick it up and saw that it was a photograph. Without meaning to pry into Frank's affairs, he glanced at the picture as he straightened up, and his breath stopped.

It was a photo of him with Linc, both of them naked, locked in an embrace that left nothing to the imagination. Dennis stared, frozen in horror, at the picture. They would never have allowed anyone to be present when they were having sex, let alone take their pictures. How could this have happened?

He looked up angrily as Frank came back into the room. Frank's eyes widened as he saw what Dennis held in his hand.

"What the hell does this mean?" Dennis demanded, flinging the photograph down on the surface of the table. "Where did you get this? And how?"

Frank sighed wearily and went past him into the diminutive kitchen, busying himself with the coffee pot. The water ran at the sink for a moment.

"I'm sorry you saw that," he said without turning. "I promised Linc I would never let anyone know about it."

"Linc knew about this?" Dennis was incredulous. "I can't believe that. He would have told me."

"He might have, when you arrived," Frank said. "He never had that chance."

"But, surely he didn't...he didn't condone something like this. It's dirty. It's awful."

Frank looked over his shoulder at him. "Don't you get it, Dennis?" he asked. "Linc was being blackmailed?"

Dennis sat in frozen silence. Blackmail? Of course, that explained everything: the missing money, why he should have been at a sleazy bar like The Ship's Call. It even explained his date with Jeff.

"I should have figured that out," he said quietly, his anger fading to be replaced by a heavy sadness.

"He came to see me about the pictures," Frank said, returning from the stove and resting a gentle hand on Dennis' shoulder.

"Pictures? You mean there are more of them?"

"About a dozen, as I recall. That's the only one I held on to. He asked me what I thought he should do. I told him he should go to the police, but apparently he went ahead with his appointment to meet his blackmailer. You know the result."

"But you should have told the police about this," Dennis said vehemently.

"Should I?" Frank asked. "Linc gave his life trying to keep those pictures from becoming a scandal, from ruining not just his life, but yours, and your military career. And think what it would have done to his family, to his father, with his bad heart. Did I have any right to cause all that harm, to ruin his reputation and yours by bringing this into the open, when he had made me vow not to say anything? His murderer will be found, and he will be punished for Linc's murder, hopefully without the blackmail every entering into it. Bringing all this into the open won't help Linc any."

Dennis leaned his head in his hands. "I suppose you're right," he said helplessly. Blackmail and murder—Linc had gone to The Ship's Call to meet the person who was blackmailing him. It was clear, too, that the one who had been blackmailing him was the same one who had murdered him. And Dennis suspected that he knew who that blackmailer was.

"I met Jeff," he said wearily, without looking up.

Frank had been in the act of bringing two cups of coffee to the table. The cups rattled in their saucers. "You did what?" he demanded loudly.

"I met Jeff. I know who he is, the young man Linc went to meet at The Ship's Call," Dennis said.

"But where, how?" Frank asked, setting the coffee on the table. "Don't tell me you've been playing detective?"

Dennis nodded. "I had to know the truth. I went to The Ship's Call and met a man there who calls himself Sandy, but his real name is Jeff. I heard one of his friends call him that, and I saw the name on some letters in his apartment. Jeff Conrad."

His voice a dull monotone, he told Frank all of it, about his trip to The Ship's Call, about meeting Sandy and going home with him, the letters, and about Sandy's brother, Don.

"You went to his apartment, knowing he might be a murderer?" Frank said, astonished. "Good god, and there were two of them there at one time. You might have been killed yourself, you little fool. You're lucky; to be here."

Not so lucky, Dennis thought, remembering Sandy with his radiant grin and his beautifully sculpted body; Sandy who, only a few hours earlier, he had held in his arms and kissed tenderly. He felt his heart was about to break.

"I had to know," he said aloud.

"Well, you can't see them again," Frank said. "It's too dangerous."

Dennis looked up at him. "But I have to, don't you see? If Sandy killed Linc, I have to find some way to prove that. We owe Linc that, both of us."

Frank was silent for a moment, studying him somberly. "I suppose you're right at that," he said. "Okay, then, but if you insist upon making a hero of yourself, I insist on helping. At least there will be two of us against two of them."

"When the time comes, I will be more than glad for your help," Dennis said. "But, I can't very well take you along as a chaperone when I go to see Sandy. Don't worry, I'll be careful, more so than ever. But I really don't think he suspects anything. And when the pieces are all fitted together, we'll both get into it."

"I still don't like it," Frank said, sipping his coffee. "But if that's the way you want it, I'll go along with you, for the moment, anyway. But I'm not saying I won't take matters into my own hands if I think it's necessary. For one thing, I want to have this fellow's address, just in case anything should happen. As it is now, if you just disappeared, I wouldn't even have a clue where to start looking."

Dennis told him Sandy's address, which Frank wrote carefully on a slip of paper. "I don't know his brother, Don's address, but I can probably find that out," Dennis said.

"It probably would be a good idea if you did," Frank said. "If these two are the ones we are looking for, that shouldn't be too hard to prove. One of them must still have some of these pictures in his possession."

Dennis nodded his head. "You're right, there should be copies of the pictures, or at least the negatives. If I had only known about them before—I'm sorry, I know that you promised Linc, and I could see why he wouldn't want anyone to know about this, although I feel sure he would have told me when I got here."

"Probably so," Frank agreed, but he did not sound altogether convinced. "At any rate, we'll never really know."

Dennis picked up the picture again and stared at it in disgust. "I can't understand how this could have been taken, without our knowing it."

Frank shrugged. "I'm afraid I can't help you with that. I don't know a thing about photography."

"I don't even know where it was taken," Dennis went on. "We're on a twin bed, and you can see the corner of another one there in the background, but Linc's apartment has one king size bed in the bedroom."

"We'll find out all that when we find the other pictures. They may show more of the room, thought that may not help much," Frank said. "These people are obviously professionals, and I'm sure they have all sorts of tricks. I've heard that a good photographer can combine pictures. For all we know, you might not have been on a twin bed in reality. For that matter, this might not even be you and Linc, just your faces, and somebody else's bodies."

Dennis looked at the picture more closely. Linc's face, in fact, was not visible from the camera angle, only enough of it to convince Dennis that it was Linc. And he could not be mistaken about that body, he knew it too well. As for himself, however, he was plainly recognizable from head to toe.

"No, it's us," he said, shoving the photograph away as if it were contaminated. "But the background could have been changed. Superimposed, I think they call it."

Frank picked up the picture from the table. "I'd better put this away somewhere safe," he said, "We don't want anyone else seeing it."

"Can't we tear it up? Or burn it?"

"No, we may need it to give to the police. That might turn out to be the only way to see things resolved."

"I guess you're right," Dennis said, standing. "But I promise you one thing: if there is any way of proving that these two murdered Linc, I'll find it."

He was sincere, but he knew unfortunately that there was a certain amount of bravado to his promise. He was determined to get to the bottom of all this, but at the moment he had no concrete idea as to how he was going to find the answers he sought—or even what he was going to do when he found them.

GOODBYE, MY LOVER, BY VICTOR J. BANIS

CHAPTER SEVEN
◊

Still dazed by what he had learned from Frank, Dennis started back to Beverly Hills. Some nagging question lingered at the back of his mind as he drove, but he could not summon it to his consciousness. He felt too weary and beaten down just at the moment to think clearly. There could no longer be any doubt in his mind. Sandy—beautiful and sexy and, yes, charming though he was—was in fact a despicable creature who would stop at nothing to gain his own ends. He had committed blackmail and murder, and God only knew what other crimes.

Somehow, he had to search Sandy's apartment, to find the evidence that he needed. There must be copies of the pictures, as Frank had pointed out, or certainly the negatives. He would have to find some way of doing it when Sandy was out, when there was no likelihood of his being discovered, as he very nearly had before.

He suddenly slapped his hand against the steering wheel. Of course, Sandy had planned to be out today. He was going to meet his brother. If he could only somehow get inside Sandy's apartment...he turned at the next corner and headed toward Sandy's apartment instead of Linc's.

He was almost there when he saw a drugstore. He pulled over to the curb, and went inside in search of a pay phone. There was an ominous wait as the phone rang—once, twice—and then he heard Sandy's voice on the other end of the line.

"Hi," he said, fighting to keep the disappointment from his voice. "I was in your neighborhood and thought maybe you might be home after all."

"Come on, tell the truth," Sandy said in a teasing voice, "You just can't stay away from me."

"Well, since you ask," Dennis forced a laugh. "You're right. Would you like some company? Or were you going out?"

"Sure, I'd love company, and I'm not going out until later. Don was here but he left a little while ago and I'm all by my lonesome. Come on over."

Dennis left the phone booth more discouraged than ever. Now he was committed to stopping by at Sandy's, and he would not have the hoped-for opportunity to search the place.

He started to leave the drugstore, and stopped just inside the door as Sandy's brother, Don, passed on the sidewalk outside. He thought of the interest Don had shown in him the night before, when he was leaving Sandy's.

He had used his physical appeal to gain Sandy's confidence, hadn't he? Maybe that was an answer: play up to Don also; work both ends against the middle. It was a gamble, a dangerous one, but there was a possibility it might work. He pushed through the door of the drugstore. Don was a half a block away by this time, his back to him.

"Don, hey," he called after him.

To his surprise, Don went on without pausing. Dennis took a step in that direction and opened his mouth to call again, and stopped instead, pondering. The sidewalk was not crowded, and he knew that his voice was the sort that carried well. By all rights, Don should have heard him, and should have paused at least to look back. That was the natural, even the instinctive, reaction to hearing someone call one's name, wasn't it? Unless—this thought came to him out of the blue—unless the name were not terribly familiar to you—a name, perhaps, that one hadn't been using for very long…a name that really wasn't your name.

The answer was suddenly clear to him. He had overheard the name Jeff in the conversation between Sandy and the old man at the bar, and he had assumed the old man was addressing Sandy at the time, but they could just as easily have been talking about someone else…about Sandy's brother, maybe.

The letter at the apartment, too, it had been addressed to Jeff—but it was not improbable that Sandy might receive mail for his brother. Particularly if his brother was laying low.

Dennis stared after the figure retreating into the distance. Don, of course—who looked a bit like his brother, only rougher, cruder—who fitted perfectly the description of the stranger Linc had met, not Sandy. Don was the Jeff for whom he had been searching.

On an impulse, Dennis started after him. At this distance, it was unlikely Jeff would recognize him even if he turned around, and it was an opportunity, perhaps the only one he would have, to find out where Jeff lived.

He darted into a doorway as he saw Jeff stop. When he looked again, Jeff was gone. He hurried on, praying that luck was with him. Which doorway, he asked himself frantically? He got to the approximate spot where he had last seen Jeff, but it was impossible to say into what door he had entered. Small shops lined the street. One of them was a pawnshop. He was sure that Jeff had been near the pawnshop, but there were other doors on either side of it. Jeff might have gone through either one of them.

He opened one of the doors next to the pawnshop and stepped inside, to find himself in the vestibule of an apartment building, at the foot of steep stairs. The area was dark and musty. To his right, just inside the door, was a small cluster of mailboxes. He leaned close to read the names in the dim light: Adams, Crandon, Conrad, Brothers…his eyes went back to Conrad. That was it, wasn't it? The name on that letter in Sandy's apartment had been Conrad, Jeff Conrad, he was sure of it. Of course, Conrad wasn't an unusual name, but surely it was too much of a coincidence to think that another Conrad lived in the very same building Jeff had just entered.

Above him, a door opened. With a quick movement, Dennis was at the front door and outside again. He stepped to the window of the pawnshop and, holding his breath, pretended to study the things on display: a drum set, a tabletop television, a set of encyclopedias.

The door through which he had just exited opened and an elderly lady came out. Dennis breathed a sigh of relief, and started off down the street. Sandy was expecting him, and he could hardly search Jeff's apartment with him in it, but at least he knew now where it was. The only problem that remained was how to get inside it, alone, but hopefully he had a solution for that, too.

It was only a few blocks to Sandy's apartment. He left the Mercedes parked where it was and walked. As he rounded the corner down from Sandy's building, he saw Frank's Cadillac parked at the curb outside and his spirits lifted. Good old Frank—true to his word, he was keeping his eyes on everyone. Even if things should get rough later, Frank would be close at hand to help him out of any jam. Knowing that relieved much of his anxiety.

He thought about what he had just learned about Jeff, who was really Don and not Sandy. Yes, Frank should know about that, too, and he should know Jeff's address. Dennis could see Frank sitting behind the wheel of the car, and he started toward it. He half lifted his hand to wave and attract Frank's attention, but on an impulse, he glanced up. Sandy was standing at his window, looking down. Dennis waved to him instead and walked past Frank's car. He caught a quick glance from Frank as he went by but he gave no sign of recognition as he started up the steps to Sandy's apartment.

GOODBYE, MY LOVER, BY VICTOR J. BANIS

CHAPTER EIGHT
◇

"Boy, you're as jumpy as a cat today," Sandy said.

Dennis forced his mouth into a smile. "Sorry," he said, reaching out to squeeze Sandy's arm affectionately. "I had something on my mind."

Sandy shrugged and lit a cigarette. "Well, I guess you can't be romantic all the time."

Dennis forced himself to move closer and put his arm around Sandy's shoulders. He couldn't afford to alienate Sandy now, not at this crucial stage. "I'll be better tonight, I promise," he said.

Sandy frowned. "Damn, I forgot," he said, "I'll be a little late tonight. Don's coming by here later. He needed some money and I didn't have any on hand, so I told him I'd go to the bank. He's stopping by to pick it up about nine or nine thirty, so I can meet you after that, okay?"

Dennis barely suppressed his excitement. "Sure, I don't mind," he said quickly, hoping he didn't sound too eager. This was the chance he wanted, when he was certain Jeff would be out of his apartment for a while. He would be free to go through it, to find the pictures.

"Look, I'd better go," he said, standing up from the sofa. "The guy I'm staying with loaned me his car and I promised I'd get it back to him early."

Sandy stood too. "You're sure there isn't something bothering you?" he asked, gazing intently into Dennis' eyes. "You've been in a funny mood this afternoon, ever since you got here."

Dennis laughed and put his arms around his companion. "Maybe," he said, "It's because I'm afraid of you."

Sandy's eyebrows went up. "Afraid of me?"

"Afraid of my feelings for you." That at least was the truth.

Sandy smiled and returned the embrace. "Don't be," he said tenderly. "If you must know, the feeling is mutual. I only wish..." He checked himself without finishing. "But that's enough mush. Go on, get your car back. I'll see you later tonight."

As he left, Dennis saw with disappointment that Frank's car was gone. He had hoped to share his new information with him. He glanced at his watch: three o'clock. There was still plenty of time to get in touch with Frank before he went to Jeff's apartment.

He called Frank when he returned home, but there was still no answer, nor was there when he tried again an hour later. Of course, it was possible that Frank might think he was still at Sandy's apartment. Maybe he had only left for a few minutes, to get himself some coffee or something, and had come back to keep his vigil without knowing that Dennis was no longer there.

The afternoon dragged by slowly, seeming like an eternity. Eight o'clock came at last. Dennis dressed for The Ship's Call. He tried Frank's number one more time, still without an answer, and left the apartment.

On a hunch, he drove to Frank's apartment and tried the bell, without success. He found a scrap of paper in the glove compartment and wrote Jeff's name and address on it, and shoved the note under Frank's door. That was the best he could do under the circumstances, but at least Frank would know where he was going. Then he set out for Jeff's.

It was not quite nine when he parked across the street from the building in which Jeff lived. He sat in the car for a minute or two, wondering whether he could safely assume that Jeff was already out. As if on cue, Jeff emerged from the building and set off walking down the street, in the direction of Sandy's.

Dennis waited until he had turned a corner and vanished from sight before he got out of the car. Inside the building, he paused to check the number of Jeff's apartment. Then, his heart in his throat, he started up the steep stairs. The boards creaked beneath his feet, the sound loud and ominous to his ears. At the top, he found the right door, and glanced up and down the hall to make sure there was no one around. Then he opened his pocketknife and knelt down in front of the lock.

It was the old-fashioned kind, as he had hoped. As a youngster, he and a friend had made a game of picking locks. He doubted that he could do anything with the newer, modern locks, but hopefully his childhood skills would work on this one.

He worked the thin blade around inside the lock, listening intently, sweating and glancing occasionally up and down the hall. After what seemed a lifetime, his efforts were rewarded with a telltale click. He turned the knob, and the door swung open.

Once inside, he paused for a moment to get his bearings. He had forgotten to bring a flashlight. Probably there was one in the car, but time was precious. He crossed to the windows and pulled the dusty curtains closed over them, and gambled on switching on a table lamp.

It was not much of an apartment. The walls were covered with dirty wallpaper that hung loose in several sections. A battered chest of drawers stood against one wall, with a hot plate and a coffee pot sitting on top of it. Through an open doorway he could see an outdated bathroom, and behind him was the bed, an old fashioned one with iron railings at both the head and the foot and a worn coverlet spread across its surface.

At least the search would not take long. He went to the chest of drawers first and opened the top drawer. There was nothing there but socks and some jockey shorts, and a couple of jockstraps that looked in need of washing.

There were shirts in the drawer below that. He was about to close it when his eyes fell on the corner of a manila envelope sticking out from under the shirts. With shaking hands he took the envelope out of the drawer, careful not to disarrange the shirts, and opening it, slid its contents out.

His search was ended. It was the pictures he was searching for, six of them in all, including a duplicate of the one that Frank had shown him. He thumbed quickly through them. They were all of them of him with Linc, and all as filthy and disgusting as the one he had seen.

It occurred to him how lucky he had been that Jeff and Sandy had not recognized him from the photographs. His face showed in all of them except one. He looked at them more closely. Of course, it had been a year ago, and he had changed some since then. He had been considerably thinner, for one thing; it was only it the last year that he had gotten serious about building up his body—since, the thought flashed through his mind, he had become sexually involved with Linc. His hair had been in a crew cut then, too, and it was longer now. And he wasn't exactly posing for a camera portrait. He was kissing Linc in a couple of them, and in some his facial features were contorted as he gave Linc oral pleasure, and in one his head was thrown back, a violent grimace on his face as he obviously reached an orgasm. No, if you knew it was him, he was easy to recognize, but unless one were looking for the resemblance, it would not be obvious; and, of course, though there were other details of his anatomy that could be identified by someone familiar with them, Jeff had only seen him with his clothes on, and couldn't know them.

A vague suspicion occurred to him. He studied the pictures again, and realized something he hadn't grasped before: Linc's face was not actually visible in any of them. No more than a mere glimpse, often hidden by Dennis' body. He was there, of course, in all the photographs, and Dennis could readily identify him; but a stranger wouldn't be able to. Posed and shot as they were, these photographs would have represented little threat to Linc.

They would have been a threat to him, however. It was he who was being blackmailed, through Linc, and Linc had paid, not to protect himself, but to protect Dennis.

The realization left him shaken. His legs threatened to give out under him, and he sank into a chair, staring into the gloom of the apartment. Yes, of course, he was a likely target for blackmail: a good family, a military career at stake. And Linc— Linc whose love he had not been able to believe— had paid with his life to protect someone he loved.

Now he could see it a little more clearly, at least, understand things better. It was the kind of thing Linc would have done, protecting him in this way. He could feel tears of gratitude, mingled with remorse, shame and regret, welling up inside him. It was as if Linc had shielded Dennis' body with his own and taken a bullet meant for him.

Navy training had prepared him at least for thoughts of death, of saving a shipmate or being saved by one—and in his dreams and fantasies during training he had seen himself as both a hero, and as one who was saved by the quick thinking or sacrifice of another.

This was no dream, though; this was no training exercise. Linc had died for him, in the truest sense.

At that moment, he loved Linc more than at any time when he had been alive, when they had been together, or during their yearlong separation.

But why Linc? The question intruded itself on his thoughts. Why had they gone to Linc with the pictures, and not come directly to him; or had the plan to blackmail both of them separately, and their plan simply gone awry?

No, there was another, more likely explanation: they did not know him, obviously, hadn't known where to find him.

He shook his head. That didn't make sense either when he thought about it for another minute. If they didn't know him, didn't know who he was, how would they have known that he had anything to lose? He might have just been some boyfriend of Linc's, without the money to pay blackmail.

He heard a noise in the hall—the creak of a board as someone passed the door of the apartment. It reminded him that time was swiftly passing. He shoved the pictures back into their envelope, got up from the chair where he was sitting and closed the dresser drawer again. There would be time enough later to puzzle over these questions. For now, he had been here too long already. It wouldn't take Jeff any time to walk from here to Sandy's apartment and back again. He might be returning at any moment, and it could be fatal to be caught with the pictures in his possession.

He had just started to turn toward the door when the blow struck. The room seemed to explode, and he plunged into an abyss of blackness.

GOODBYE, MY LOVER, BY VICTOR J. BANIS

CHAPTER NINE
◊

Consciousness returned to Dennis slowly and painfully. He tried to lift his hand to his head but his hand refused to move. It was a moment longer before he realized his hands were tied.

He opened one eye. Strong cords held his hands to the opposite ends of the iron headboard railing of Jeff's bed. He was flat on his stomach—and he was naked. His clothes had been stripped from him. He tried his legs and discovered that they were tied to the other end of the bed. He was spread-eagled atop the bed.

"Glad to see you wake up," a voice said above him. A pair of Levi-clad legs came into his line of vision. Dennis managed to turn his head enough to look up into Jeff's smiling face.

"Why, didn't you expect me to wake up?" he asked sarcastically. His head felt as though a thousand hammers were pounding inside it.

Jeff shrugged. "So I hit you a little harder than I intended," he said, sounding not at all apologetic. "You look pretty muscular, like you're in pretty good shape. I didn't want to have you put up a fight till I got you tied down."

"And you couldn't tie me down without taking my clothes off?" Dennis asked.

Jeff laughed out loud. "Oh, that," he said. "Well, now, to be honest, I was wondering ever since I saw you over at my brother's place how you would look in the raw, that pretty little butt of yours especially, which truly did give me some great ideas. So I just figured, this was as good a chance as any to get a look at it."

"Okay, so you've had yourself a good look" Dennis said. "So, why don't we put my clothes back on, all right?"

"Only, see, I couldn't do that without untying you, could I?" Jeff said. "And I'm not ready to do that yet. Besides, having seen it, I have to say it looks damned hot, even better than I imagined it would. Of course, if you're embarrassed, you being buck naked, and me having all my clothes on, I can always join you."

Dennis watched with angry eyes as Jeff undid his belt buckle and began on the buttons of his fly. It didn't take much guesswork to know what was coming next. He struggled against the ropes that held him.

"I can still yell," he warned.

"Don't try it," Jeff said sternly. "I'd just have to belt you again. We could keep that up all night, and that doesn't sound like much fun for either of us."

He stooped to remove his boots, and straightened again. His T-shirt came up over his head, and he tossed it aside. He caught his thumbs in the waist of his Levis and began to peel them slowly downward.

He wore nothing underneath. Despite his fear, Dennis watched him strip as though mesmerized, his heart pounding. Jeff was a big man, taller and considerably heavier than Sandy. His brawny body was black with hair, his chest barrel-sized, his legs, only inches from Dennis' face just now, like thick columns of hairy granite.

"Not bad, huh?" Jeff asked, looking down at himself.

Embarrassed, Dennis had avoided looking in that direction, but now he followed Jeff's glance downward, and shuddered as he tried to imagine himself accommodating what he saw. Jeff had bragged before about how big he was. He hadn't been kidding. Dennis closed his eyes against the sight. He had surrendered his virginity to Sandy, and after the first time or two it hadn't been terribly painful; but he knew that he wasn't ready for anything like this.

Jeff laughed again, and the bed sagged as he knelt upon it, over Dennis' helpless body. He fell upon Dennis roughly, his enormous weight crushing the breath from Dennis' lungs.

"Damn you," Dennis gasped hoarsely. His further protests were muffled as a pillow was shoved into his face.

The attack was mercilessly cruel, without preamble or preparations. Jeff entered him without pause, driving deeply into him, and began at once to ride him savagely. Dennis felt as though he were being torn asunder with each vicious stroke. His body shook with agony and humiliation, and his futile struggles only seemed to incite his attacker to even more violent efforts.

"That's what a real man feels like, baby," Jeff said breathlessly into his ear. He bit into the flesh of Dennis shoulder, drawing blood, and his huge hands grasped Dennis' slender hips roughly to force him closer as he continued his pile drivers.

Dennis prayed for unconsciousness that would spare him the pain of the assault, but he remained all too conscious of what was happening. It seemed to go on forever, an eternity since it had begun. His body was limp now, burning with the crazed thrusts of the man atop him, ramrodding him with pause. Again and again Jeff slammed himself against and into the yielding softness of Dennis' bottom.

It ended at last in a burst of rampant savagery as Jeff not only pounded into him but clawed and bit at him, his tempo mounting to a lightening pace. With a loud groan, he reached his finish and collapsed over the bruised and battered body beneath him.

Dennis lay motionless and defeated as Jeff rose and made his way to the bathroom. He came back a few minutes later, lifting the pillow away from Dennis' face, and knelt beside the bed.

"How're you feeling?" he asked, still grinning.

"Sore," Dennis said angrily. "Mentally and physically."

Far from acting sorry, Jeff threw back his head and laughed loudly. Growing sober again, he found some cigarettes on the nightstand and lit one. To Dennis amazement, Jeff offered him a puff.

116

"Okay," Jeff said finally, "So you got butt raped. Face it, kid, you had it coming. If you want to play with fire, you can't squeal when you get burnt. Now, I want some answers. What the hell were you doing searching my room? You a cop?"

"No," Dennis answered coldly. "Since you ask, I was Lincoln Gardner's lover."

That statement had its effect. "Gardner? You mean…?"

"I mean, the man you murdered," Dennis finished for him.

Jeff stood abruptly and reached for a switchblade atop the dresser. It sprang open with a click that sounded loud in the stillness. "I'm pretty good with this," he told Dennis, showing him the knife.

Dennis closed his eyes again. This was it, then, the moment he had gambled with. But even if he died, Jeff would still get his. Frank knew where he was, and Frank knew who Jeff was. Jeff would not get away with his murder.

To his surprise, the tension on his legs lessened. He opened his eyes and realized Jeff had cut them loose. His hands were next, and in another moment he was free. Jeff stood back from the bed, the knife in his hand, watching him cautiously.

"You can sit up," he said, "But no funny business, okay?"

"Okay," Dennis said. He sat up stiffly, rubbing his wrists where the rope had cut into them. He looked at Jeff and saw that he still held the knife at the ready.

"Now what?" Dennis asked. "I suppose you want to work on the other side?"

"Not a bad idea, now that you mention it," Jeff said. "But not just now, thank you. Now we talk. Are you the kid in the pictures?" Dennis nodded. "I'll be damned. I knew there was something familiar about you, but I never figured on that. Hell, I should have recognized those cute little buns. There can't be another set as sweet as those babies." He picked up the pictures and looked at them, and back at Dennis. "You've changed since these were taken, though."

"Who took them, you?" Dennis asked. This was his one chance to find out the answers to his question. Jeff hadn't killed him yet. Maybe he still would, but maybe at least before then, he could learn what he wanted to know, the answers to his questions.

Jeff shook his head. "Me?" He laughed dryly. "No, I'm not a photographer. As a matter of fact, I didn't even see the pictures until after the business with Gardner."

Dennis gave a mocking laugh. "That's pretty hard to believe. You were blackmailing him with them, weren't you? You killed him over them."

"Like hell I did," Jeff exclaimed, serious now. "Yeah, I figured it was blackmail, but I was getting well paid to act as a messenger. Believe it or not, that's all I was. I was to meet Gardner at the bar, go with him to his place, and swap envelopes. I wasn't told anything about what was in the envelopes, just to swap them with Gardner, and bring the other one back to the bar. When we got to Gardner's apartment, though, he started talking about pictures, said he wanted them, and the negatives. I told him I didn't know anything about any pictures. When he found out that I was just a messenger for someone else, he told me the deal was off. He said to tell the guy that had sent me that unless he had the pictures by morning, without paying, he was going to the police. I delivered his message, and the next thing I knew, he was dead.'

Dennis sat for a moment, trying to absorb this unexpected information. "Who did you deliver the message to?" he asked finally. "Who was your boss?"

Jeff shook his head vehemently. "Forget it," he said. "I'm not saying who it was."

"But don't you see, whoever it was must have murdered Linc?"

"Sure, I know that. But look at it this way: the police are looking for me, right? And do you think they're going to believe me if I go to them with my story? Like hell they will. I'll be on my way to the gas chamber in no time at all, that's what they do with murderers here in California. Oh, no, there's only one thing that'll clear me, and that's a confession from the man who did it."

"And how do you think you're going to get that?" Dennis asked.

"I don't know," Jeff said. "But I'll think of something."

Dennis looked at the knife again, and back to Jeff's face. "Damn it," he said with a weary sigh, "The crazy things is, I believe you."

"Can I put this away, then?" Jeff asked, brandishing the knife.

"You'd make me a lot happier if you would."

The knife clicked shut and bounced onto the top of the dresser. "You better get your clothes on,"

Jeff told him, and added with a sly smile, "Unless you feel like another session. I could always use some more of that, and like you said, I haven't even got around to what you've got hanging there, and that looks pretty good too."

Despite himself, Dennis had to laugh begrudgingly. "No, thanks," he said, reaching for his clothes. "I've had enough of your brand of sex for one evening.

Jeff sat and watched him with frank interest as he dressed. Dennis' body was still sore from his assault, and he found himself moving slowly and painfully.

"You know," he said when he had finished dressing, "I could still go to the police and tell them all about you."

"And I could stop you if I wanted to," Jeff reminded him, nodding his head in the direction of the knife.

"You could," Dennis agreed, "But you won't. You had your chance to do that a few minutes ago."

Jeff grinned and nodded. "Yeah, right. I may rape a nice looking guy, especially when I catch him snooping around in my room, but I don't go for cutting them up." He grew sober again. "Look, at least do me one favor: give me a little time to see if I can straighten things out, okay?"

Dennis hesitated. He did owe him something for sparing his life; and, however bizarre it sounded, he really did believe Jeff was telling him the truth. "How long?" he asked.

"Give me until tomorrow, anyway. I'll see what I can do tonight, okay? I'm supposed to meet…I'm meeting with somebody later, and I'm going to try to talk some sense into him."

"Okay," Dennis said. "I'll get I touch with you tomorrow. But, after that, I can't promise to keep quiet."

"Okay, I'll go with that." Jeff extended his hand, and, after a moment, Dennis took it. "No bad feelings?" Jeff asked.

Dennis smiled ruefully and gingerly rubbed his backside. "I'll let you know tomorrow," he said. "We may still have a score to settle between us."

Jeff laughed again. "Fair enough. How about a beer before you go?" he offered. "To show there's no hard feelings?"

"I could use something," Dennis said. "Got any Scotch?"

"Never drink the stuff. I got some beer in the fridge, though."

Dennis was about to accept when he suddenly remembered Sandy, waiting for him at The Ship's Call. "Holy smoke," he cried, "What time is it?"

"About eleven," Jeff said.

"I'd better pass on that beer," Dennis said, heading for the door. "I was supposed to meet Sandy an hour ago."

"Hey," Jeff called as he started out the door. Dennis paused and looked back. Jeff was still naked, his awesome endowments on blatant display.

"About that score you said we had to settle," he said with a wink, "That's okay by me, too, any time you're in the mood. I'm a give and take kind of guy, you know what I mean?"

GOODBYE, MY LOVER, BY VICTOR J. BANIS

CHAPTER TEN
◇

As Dennis closed Jeff's door behind him, a woman opened her door across the hall. Dennis turned his head away from the curious glance she gave him and hurried down the dark stairs. Despite his discomfort, he could not help smiling to himself as he reached the bottom. It had been a harrowing experience, one that, for a while there, he had not expected to live through, but here he was with nothing worse than a few aches and an aching backside—and in all fairness, as Jeff had pointed out, he had sort of asked for that.

His anger had been forgotten in his relief at still being alive, and his elation over all that he had learned. He had no difficulty believing Jeff's story. After all, if Jeff really had been a murderer, he could have killed him while he had him tied up helplessly, and maybe he could have even successfully covered his tracks.

When he got to his car, however, his thoughts grew somber again. If Jeff had only been a messenger for someone else, someone who really had murdered Linc, there was one obvious answer to who that person was. He was back to Sandy again as his prime suspect. It was certainly natural that Jeff should want to cover up for his own brother, wasn't it?

Should he go ahead with his date with Sandy; or was it time to turn the whole problem over to the police, to Mathews? He had the pictures—his hand went automatically to his pocket. No, the pictures were gone, Jeff had taken them while he was unconscious, and they were still back there in his apartment.

He frowned and paused to light a cigarette. He had promised Jeff that he would wait for another day; but he would have to see Jeff before he went to the police. Without Jeff, and without the photographs, he actually had nothing to support his story. He thought about going back to ask if he could have the pictures, and decided he would give Jeff till tomorrow, as he had promised. Anyway, he was really late, and Sandy was waiting at the bar.

He had just reached for the ignition switch when he heard the sound of breaking glass, and a woman nearby on the sidewalk screamed. He looked in her direction. A small crowd of people was already gathering across the street, in front of Jeff's apartment building.

Afraid of what he would find, Dennis jumped from the car and dashed back across the street, dodging the traffic.

He saw Jeff before he reached the spot. The burly man was dressed only in his Levis, which he must have put back on after Dennis had left. The twisted position in which he lay sprawled on the sidewalk, his head at an impossible angle to his shoulders, left no hope that he might have survived the fall from above.

Dennis stood horror stricken, staring at the man he had just left, whose body had been intimately linked with his just minutes before. Was this Jeff's way out, his way of escaping that gas chamber he had mentioned? He had hardly seemed the type for suicide, and surely he had not been in that kind of mood. He had joked about another sexual encounter as Dennis was leaving. Men who were about to commit suicide surely didn't try to get a partner interested in sexual activity. Or was it an accident, had he simply stumbled and fallen through the window? Or, maybe it was something more sinister?

"He must have fallen," someone said for the crowd.

"Small wonder," a woman said. "He smells like a brewery. He was probably staggering around up there, and lost his balance, and fell through the window."

The rest of the excited conversation ran together as the implications of what they were saying sank into Dennis' mind. Jeff had not been drinking a few minutes earlier. He might have gotten himself a beer after Dennis had gone, but he could hardly have gotten drunk in that space of time. Someone must have wanted it to appear that Jeff was drunk, and if someone had tried to create that impression, then it meant that someone else had caused the fall. Someone who had been in the apartment when he was, or immediately after he left.

"He had a friend in there with him," the woman was telling the crowd. "A young blond fellow. He just left there a few minutes ago, I saw him go out the door."

Dennis swore silently to himself. It was the woman who had seen him leaving Jeff's apartment; but, surely, he could not be suspect, could he?

But why not, he asked himself helplessly? Even if the entire story came out, the blackmail and all, it would certainly look as though he had come here seeking revenge for Linc's murder. What else would anyone think?

He half turned to go, and stopped again as his eyes fell on a familiar figure who suddenly stepped from the crowd and knelt down beside Jeff's lifeless body. The face was turned away from him at the moment, but he would have recognized Sandy in any crowd. Had he been upstairs as well?

Moving slowly and as inconspicuously as possible, Dennis made his way through the crowd and back to the corner, crossed the street when the light changed, and forced himself to walk nonchalantly back to his car. With each passing second, he waited to hear the shout of recognition that he was sure would come.

There was no shout, however, and a few minutes later, he was driving slowly in the late evening traffic, headed in the direction of Linc's apartment.

There was no point now in going to the bar to meet Sandy.

* * * * * * *

126

Back at the apartment, Dennis poured himself a stiff drink to try to calm his nerves. He was at a complete loss as to what he should do next. The situation had suddenly blown up in his face. Now, instead of just one murder, there were two, and he was very much involved in one of them. His attempts at playing detective had cost Jeff his life and had landed him in a precarious spot.

He thought of Frank and tried once again to call him at his apartment, but there still was no answer there. He needed to talk to Frank, to get someone else's advice. Things were out of his hands now, beyond his control.

He paced nervously to the window and stared down at the street, trying to think clearly again. Obviously Jeff had been murdered, and an attempt had been made to look it look like an accident, or possibly suicide. If the attempt had been successful, it would have meant that the murderer had gotten away with two killings. Surely the killer, whoever he was, would have taken the incriminating photographs as well. There would no longer be any trail to Linc's murder.

There was only one likely suspect for Jeff's murder. It must have been Sandy whom Jeff was protecting; and Sandy had been right there, at the scene. But if the police concluded that Jeff had been murdered, then Dennis himself was the one person they were most likely to suspect. He had the motive, and he had the opportunity. A witness had seen him leave the apartment. It wouldn't be hard for Mathews to deduce who the young blond was.

What if he took the initiative and went to the police, to Mathews, now? Would the policeman be-

127

lieve his story about blackmail, with no evidence to support it? It was unlikely, without at least the picture Frank still had. And in any event, going to the police with that story meant opening that Pandora's box, the door to scandal, not only for Linc and his family, but for himself as well, and his family, and surely the end of his military career.

A car rounded the corner below with squealing tires and came to a quick stop outside. Dennis heart leaped into his throat when he recognized Sandy's MG. Sandy jumped from the car and started for the building.

He couldn't face Sandy now, not knowing what he did. With a quick movement, he flicked out the light and stood in darkness, scarcely able to breathe.

The bell rang, sounding shrill and ominous in the dark silence. Dennis stood frozen where he was, waiting as the bell rang again and again. Finally it stopped. Fighting back the tears in his eyes, Dennis dropped onto the sofa, his head in his hands. There was still time for Sandy to escape. Even if the police discovered his identity, he might be able to get away with his life. For a fleeting moment, Dennis almost ran after him to tell him to run.

The telephone shattered the silence. Dennis reached for it, and paused. What if it were Sandy? If he answered the phone, Sandy would be back in a moment. But it could be Frank, too, and logic told him that Sandy hadn't had time enough to reach a telephone in the few minutes since he had been at the door. Hoping, he grabbed the receiver from its cradle, and gasped with relief when he recognized Frank's voice.

"Things have gone completely haywire," he told Frank excitedly.

"I know." Frank spoke rapidly and in a subdued voice. "I heard about Jeff. He was murdered, and the police are looking for a young, blond man who was seen coming out of his apartment. That was you, wasn't it?"

"Yes, I was there," Dennis said with a break in his voice. "But he was all right when I left him, I swear it, Frank. What should I do? Should I go to the police and turn myself in?"

"No," Frank said sharply. "If you go to them now, they'll arrest you for sure and charge you with Jeff's murder. What we've got to do for now is, get you out of the picture until I have time to straighten things out. I promise you, I'll take care of everything."

"Out of the picture? You mean, run away?" Dennis asked. The suggestion sent a chill down his spine. A fugitive from the law? He had never in his wildest nightmares imagined himself in that role.

"It's just for a day or two," Frank said. "Look, you remember that shack of mine up in the mountains, up by Big Bear?"

Dennis had to think for a moment before it came back to him: he and Linc had used Frank's shack for a weekend, it seemed like an eternity ago. "Yes, I remember it," he said. "Out in the woods, off all by itself."

"I think that's where you should go," Frank said. "Just until things cool off a little."

Dennis felt numb, his thoughts all in a jumble. He no longer felt capable of thinking reasonably. The strain was too much for him, and he was grateful to leave everything to Frank. Frank sounded so calm, so reasonable. "I guess I could drive up there tonight," he said.

"No, they might get around to looking for Linc's car," Frank said. "Anyway, I don't want you by yourself just now. You're too freaked out. I'll drive you there. How soon can you be ready?"

"I'll be ready by the time you get here," Dennis said.

"I'll be there in half an hour." Frank hung up without waiting for a reply.

Dennis stood staring at the phone for a moment. So, it had come to this: running into the night like a frightened animal? But Frank was right, surely. They needed time, time for his thoughts to settle themselves, time perhaps to put together the pieces of the puzzle in some way that did not incriminate Sandy. It would only be for a day, two at the most. Shaking off his lethargy, he went for his bag and began packing it hurriedly. By the time Frank arrived, almost precisely half an hour later, he was ready to go.

"Come on, there isn't any time to waste," Frank greeted him curtly.

Only a short time later, they were in Frank's Cadillac, speeding south on the Hollywood Freeway, and from there on to the San Bernardino, that would take them out of the city and into the San Bernardino Mountains eighty miles to the east.

It was already the wee hours of the morning. The big car rode smoothly and quietly, its engine barely purring. Dennis leaned back in the comfortable seat, exhausted, and tried to sleep, but his mind continued to whirl crazily, spinning from one incredible event to another.

The traffic grew thinner and soon they were out in the open countryside, rushing past vineyards and smaller towns, mostly dark at this hour. Frank drove in silence, watching the highway grimly, and Dennis realized with a rush of gratitude and guilt that Frank had not slept either. Worse, he was placing himself in a dangerous position by helping a suspected criminal.

They passed through the city of San Bernardino and the road began to climb, winding its way upward into the mountains that stood as dark sentinels outside. The terrain grew steeper, the road more twisting. Frank reduced his speed of necessity, the car swaying at each curved. It had snowed recently, and although the road was clear, the trees along the road were laden with white.

It was nearly dawn by the time they arrived at Frank's shack in the woods. It was a cabin, really, but Frank had always called it his shack. It stood by itself at the end of a long, unpaved lane, covered now with a mantle of snow, and surrounded by pine trees and rocky crags. No one would find him here. A person could spend months here away from the world.

"You get a fire going," Frank said as he unlocked the door and led the way inside. "I'll go get us some food. There's a little general store a few miles up the road. It should be opening up about now."

Alone in the cabin, Dennis busied himself with getting a fire started. There was wood already stacked in the fireplace, and tinder and matches, and in just a few minutes he had a welcome blaze going, chasing the winter chill from the unheated room.

The cabin was minimally furnished and rustic. There were no modern conveniences. Kerosene lanterns on the mantle took the place of electric lights. He lit a couple of the lanterns, instinctively wrinkling his nose at the smell and adjusting the wicks until he had a steady light glowing. Water came from a pump in the back. He remembered that would have to be primed with hot water, and he took a pot outside and filled it with snow, and hung that over the fireplace to melt.

Standing before the fire, warming his hands from the snow, he remembered his weekend here with Linc, and how romantic it had been: the wind in the pine trees outside, the flickering light of lamps and candles in here, and the roaring fire. He looked around. The cabin was still the same, with its simple, rustic furnishings, and the upright piano against one wall, looking strangely out of place. He could almost hear Linc playing it for him, while he sat on the floor by the fireplace, rapt: Chopin, the first concerto.

He crossed the room to the piano and thumbed through the stack of music on top of it, until he found the concerto Linc had played for him that night. He seemed to hear the notes, hauntingly familiar—but there was something about the music that teased at his consciousness, something not quite right.

He remembered at last: Frank's practice records. It had been the same concerto on those records—and it had sounded so very much as though Linc were playing.

Frowning, he opened the score and looked through it, wishing now that he had paid more attention to what Linc had tried to teach him about reading music.

He found what he thought was the passage he was looking for, the place on the recordings where the pianist had trouble with the notes, and had played the section through again, and a third time.

The music that had given him trouble was written for the left hand. He remembered now that Linc had trouble with that same passage the night here, at the cabin. He had stopped here, too, and played it again. He always had trouble with his left hand, the hand that had been broken; as Frank's hand had never been broken.

It hadn't been Frank on the practice records, as he had said. It had been Linc playing the piano— playing the Chopin first concerto, and having, as he always did, trouble with the left hand passages. Frank had lied to him. But why?

Unless…He recalled something then that Mathews had told him. The neighbors had heard Linc playing the night he had been murdered. But the records had been on the phonograph, and the phonograph was one of those that shut itself off when the records were finished—so, it might have been the records that the neighbors heard, and not Linc playing the piano. Linc might already have been dead, and the records playing on the phonograph playing just to provide an alibi. Which could only mean….

Dennis raised a hand to his throbbing temples. Frank, Linc's murderer? But why, in heaven's name? That made no sense. They had always been friends.

The melody of the concerto continued to echo in his mind, as he thought back over the events of the past few days. Frank had been at The Ship's Call that night, the night of Linc's murder, according to Mathews. He had been seen there, though surely it was as unlikely a hangout for him as it had been for Linc.

At The Ship's Call, to meet his messenger, Jeff? No, the message would have been delivered earlier. But he might have gone there to establish an alibi, to be seen and to talk to people while supposedly, Linc—who in fact was already dead—entertained a trick by playing the piano.

The records had been left on the phonograph. Surely that was a foolish thing for a murderer to do, if they were his alibi. Or was it? The police would probably not question a pianist having recordings of piano music on his phonograph; and they had no reasons to be suspicious of the records. After all, they already had their own theory regarding the murder.

Other facts and pieces of information began to fall into place as his mind slowly cleared, moving back through recent time. Mathews had told him that there were two glasses in the apartment the next morning, glasses with Scotch in them. Jeff drank beer, and so did Sandy; but Frank was a Scotch drinker. Of course, many people drank Scotch; but none of them had lied to him about practice records.

He had not really until now given due thought to Linc's part in his own murder. Linc was not stupid and he was no pantywaist. He was a man of in-

134

telligence in fine physical condition. If someone had come to the apartment after Jeff had left, Linc would certainly have been on his guard, and capable of at least putting up one hell of a struggle—unless his visitor were someone he knew, someone he would never suspect, someone who came as a friend, and not as a blackmailer.

His eyes fell on his keys where he had laid them when he took off his jacket. He thought about the key that Frank had to Linc's apartment. He said Linc had given it to him, but the key on Linc's key chain hadn't fitted in the lock at his apartment. Was it possible that the keys had been switched, the murderer taking Linc's key with him so that he could return later for the phonograph records after the police were gone.

Frightened of what he might learn, Dennis picked up the ring with Linc's keys on it and stared at them for a moment. If one were going to make such a switch, and put another key on the ring in place of Linc's door key, it would surely be danger-ous to make that substitute key the one to his own apartment. One would be far more likely to leave a key instead that would not be so easily identified, one that was not so often used. One, perhaps, to a cabin in the distant mountains.

He went to the front door, opened it, and fit-ted the key into the lock there. The key turned eas-ily. Dennis dropped the keys back into his pocket.

A key to Frank's "shack" on Linc's key ring, and a key to Linc's apartment in Frank's possession. Of course, it was possible that at some time, for some reason, they had swapped the keys.

It was also becoming increasingly possible that it was Frank who had murdered Linc; and he had played right into Frank's hands by coming here with him, in the dark of the night, with no one to know where he was.

CHAPTER ELEVEN

◇

The lack of sleep and the events of the past few days were taking their toll on Dennis. He felt beaten and finished, as though he were ready to give up everything now. He was no longer sure he trusted his own thought processes.

"I've got to think clearly," he told himself stubbornly, trying to put his thoughts into some kind of logical order.

It was all crazy, too unlikely to be true. Frank could not be the murderer. Frank was Linc's oldest friend; and yet, everything fitted together so perfectly, all of those things that he should have sorted out long ago. He had been a fool from the very beginning. The shock of Linc's death was partly to blame, but he had made every mistake in the book.

At the very least, he ought to have realized when he talked to Jeff. Jeff would hardly have gone to the trouble of taking an assumed name and going into hiding to avoid his own brother, if Sandy were the killer.

Sandy—if only there were some way to reach him! But there was no phone here, he remembered that too from his previous visit, and it must be miles to the nearest house. He wouldn't even know in what direction to start hiking.

What if I'm just jumping to conclusions, he asked himself again? He stared around the room, trying to decide what he could do to be sure. Ask Frank when he returned, which surely couldn't be more than just a few minutes now? Confront him with the facts and perhaps persuade him to go to the police? He shuddered when he realized that both Linc and Jeff had contemplated that very course of action, and both of them had paid for it with their lives.

He crossed the living room and flung open the door that opened onto the diminutive bedroom, and his last doubts faded. He ought to have remembered this room, with its twin beds; he and Linc had somehow managed to make do with just one twin sized bed—though, of course, not much of their night had been spent sleeping. This was the room in the pictures. What a fool he was. He ought to have recognized the beds.

Who else but Frank could have taken the pictures? He must have come up during the one day, had arrived perhaps while he and Linc were shopping for supplies at the store down the road, or maybe while they had been hiking in the woods. He had made whatever arrangements he needed to make, a camera set up somewhere unobtrusive; maybe he had used infrared light, that was possible, though Dennis knew little about it. He and Linc had made no effort to conceal what they were doing.

138

Why should they? They had been miles from anyone who might observe them, at least so they thought, and they had clearly had no attention for anything but one another.

The brown of an envelope caught his eye and he stooped to remove it from the wastebasket; and the final confirmation fell into place. The envelope had contained photographic paper. He remembered, now, the shopping list he had found at the apartment, the list Frank had claimed as his. One of the items on the list had been photographic solution, although Frank had said that he knew nothing about photography.

He had lied from the very beginning, and Dennis had naively accepted each lie as the truth. He had led Frank right to Sandy and then to Jeff, and had ignored the evidence that had stared him in the face, crying for notice.

He started to toss the envelope back into the wastebasket, and caught himself. If the paper were here, at the shack, then this must be where Frank worked on his loathsome hobby. Photographs of the sort that he had taken could hardly be dropped off and developed at a neighborhood camera shop. Those pictures would have to be developed privately, in some safe place.

Dennis looked about the room. Frank would need a darkroom to develop and print them, that much he knew; but where would it be? The bedroom was too small and had too many windows, and there was no photographic equipment to be seen. The closets were too small, but he checked them anyway to be sure. There was nothing in the living room, or in the tiny kitchen.

He remembered, then, the shed outside: a storage shed, as Frank had told them, but he remembered that it was kept locked. Neither he nor Linc had seen inside it the weekend they had stayed here.

The shed was windowless—a perfect darkroom. It stood just outside the kitchen door, held shut with a padlock. Dennis shivered with the cold and looked around for some sort of tool. Finding nothing, he returned inside, still looking for something to force the lock.

He saw nothing in the kitchen, either, but on the hearth beside the fireplace were the tools for working the fire: a shovel, a brass poker, a dustpan and a little broom. Dennis picked up the poker, weighing it in his hand.

"This should do it," he thought, and hurried back outside. The frigid air cut through his shirt, but he was too intent on his mission to take time to go back inside for his jacket. He jammed the poker behind the padlock and pulled. For a moment the lock held. Then, with a groan, the old wood splintered and the lock came away from the door.

Dennis set the poker aside and flung the door open. This was the darkroom, all right. Even with his limited knowledge of photography, he could see that. The shed was filled with photographic equipment of all types: cameras, bulbs, tanks for solutions, even an enlarger. There were lines on which to hang the pictures to dry, and a large cabinet along one wall.

He tried one of the drawers in the cabinet and found it locked, and went back for the poker he had left in the snow outside. Impatiently, he jimmied the drawer open with the poker. There were stacks of photographs inside the drawer. He picked up a handful and looked at them. They were all of them pornographic, pictures of couples like himself and Linc, in various sexual poses and activities: naked young men, performing alone and together, a veritable library of lust.

On the bottom of the pile he found the pictures he was looking for: several prints of each shot that had been taken of himself and Linc. He shoved them into his pocket and slammed the drawer closed.

That left the negatives still unaccounted for, however. He forced open the next drawer. It was filled with stacks of negatives. He held them up toward the light from the open door, looking at them one at a time in search of the ones he needed.

"Damn," he thought suddenly, "I'm doing this the hard way. The whole idea is to destroy everything. It doesn't matter if it's Linc and me, or some other unfortunate victim of Frank's schemes."

He yanked the drawer out of the cabinet and dumped all the negatives into it. Then he removed the first drawer and stacked them together. There was still one more drawer, and he forced it open as well. It was filled with still more photographs and negatives.

He carried all three drawers back into the house and stacked them in front of the fireplace and, grabbing a handful of pictures, tossed them into the roaring fire, watching carefully to see that they all burned. When the last of them was in flames, he tossed in another handful. It would be faster, he knew, to throw them all in at once, but there were so

141

many he was afraid he might smother the fire, and he wanted to be sure that when he was finished, there was nothing left to be salvaged.

When he had completely emptied the first drawer, he tossed it roughly aside and started on the second, stopping once or twice to stir the ashes around. Whatever happened to him after this, these pictures would ruin neither Linc's good name nor anyone else's. Even if he himself were killed, or arrested for Jeff's murder, at least he would have the satisfaction of knowing he had accomplished that much.

He finished the second drawer and went to work on the third and last one. Finally, with a smile of satisfaction, he threw the last of the negatives into the fire. It was done. He was ready now to deal with the man who had taken them.

He had finished none too soon, however. He was still crouched before the fire when he felt a cold draft and suddenly realized that the door behind him was open. He looked over his shoulder, to find Frank standing in the open doorway. The angry expression on Frank's face left no doubt that he had arrived in time to realize what Dennis had done— and the gun in his hand left no doubt as to his intentions.

They remained motionless and silent for long moments, Dennis kneeling by the fireplace and Frank standing in the doorway, staring at once another. Dennis did not dare move, all too aware of the gun pointed at him. He was quite sure that Frank would not hesitate to use it.

Frank's face was flushed, his eyes glittered with evil, and his mouth was twisted in an insane smile. "So now you know," he said, breaking the silence, his voice cold and hard. "I was afraid you might start snooping around while I was gone, but I had to take the chance. I'm afraid you have sealed your fate, Dennis."

"It doesn't really make much difference, does it?" Dennis asked, meeting his gaze without flinching. "You would probably have killed me sometime anyway, sooner or later."

"Probably so," Frank said, "But I had planned on having a little more time, and some more money. And I had sort of hoped that, out of gratitude, you would have let me have a chance at that beautiful body of yours while it was still alive."

"Did you really think that was going to happen?"

Frank shrugged. "You seemed to be warming up to me. I thought we would sleep together, and I would make a pass. I felt sure you would not turn me down after all I had done for you."

"And after that?" Dennis was stalling for time, hoping that some inspiration would come to him.

"I was going to offer to help you make good your escape, out of California, out of the country, perhaps. That would have taken money, of course, quite a bit of money, you see, which I was sure you could get for me. I had counted on that money, in fact, to make good my own escape."

"Leaving me behind and dead, no doubt," Dennis said.

Frank nodded. "Oh, yes, indeed," he said, "I could hardly leave you behind to tell tales. I would have made it look like a suicide, of course, over your guilt for killing Jeff in revenge. Understand, I felt that you owed me the money, and your assistance. And some sex, too, you little tease. After all, I think it was wanting you, envying Linc the pleasure of savoring your beautiful body, that first put the idea of killing him into my mind. Besides, if it hadn't been for you and your damned snooping around, I would probably have gotten away with Linc's murder."

"Not a chance," Dennis said. He was fighting now for time, stalling until some chance presented itself to him, an opportunity to get the gun from Frank, or at least to attempt an escape. "Eventually the policed would have caught up with Jeff, even without my involvement. You don't really think he would have taken the rap for you, do you?"

"Would anyone have believed his wild story?" Frank asked. "He didn't even know who I was, or even my real name. We conducted all our business at The Ship's Call, and I have made it a point not to go back there since. He couldn't afford to go there either, afterwards, without attracting the attention of the police. Even his handsome brother had to tread softly. And what could Jeff have told the police anyway? That a stranger had approached him one night at the bar, offered him two hundred dollars to run a couple of errands? Who would have believed him? And even if the police had finally worked it out, by that time I could have been far away."

"With the money you had blackmailed form Linc? Or rather, stolen from him, when he refused to pay the blackmail. You did take the money from him when you had killed him, didn't you?"

"Of course," Frank said, looking pleased with his own cleverness. "He had it on him, the fool. But he wasn't going to pay. He told me he had decided to go to the police instead. The wonderful thing is, he told me all about it when I came by that night, never guessing that I was the one behind the blackmail scheme. I came by Linc's apartment because Jeff had told me Linc was going to the police, and I knew I had to stop him. I simply dropped by, an old friend, to have a drink. He was distressed. He ended up telling me everything...but I'm sure you've figured out the rest."

"I can understand how you did it, all right," Dennis said. He moved his foot slightly and felt the touch of cold metal, and he remembered then the poker, lying on the floor behind him. "But I can't understand the why. Why would you want to do it to Linc? He was your friend."

Frank snorted derisively. "My friend?" He spat the words out. "He was never my friend! I hated him, if you want to know the truth; I've always hated him. How do you think I felt all those years? Lincoln Gardner, the man who had everything—looks, money, talent, success, pretty young lovers—and I had nothing. I could have had a career in music, you know, I was as talented as he was, but my family didn't have his kind of money. We couldn't afford all that expensive musical education that I needed, and I ended up in the insurance business. But one thing I did, I saw to it that Linc never had a real career in music either."

As he listened and talked, Dennis lowered one hand slowly behind his leg, toward the poker that was hidden from Frank's view.

"You?" he said aloud. "You mean the accident with the piano?"

Frank laughed viciously. "How do you think a piano lid would just happen to fall?" he asked, "Unless someone had tampered with the props. Of course I caused it. I can't tell you how happy it made me, all those months he suffered—and then, when he knew he would never be able to play professionally, his grief was like music to my ears."

Dennis' fingers touched the cold metal of the poker. He strained, trying to grasp it without moving his body.

"But Linc was always generous with you," he said, "He was generous with everyone."

"Do you think I wanted to be treated like some poor relation?" Frank sneered. "No, I wanted things of my own. I wanted a lover like you. Did you know that? I hungered for you from the first moment I set eyes on you, and did you ever notice me? Not for a minute. But I told myself that if I had money, I could buy dozens like you. I wouldn't have to listen to Linc rave about how wonderful you were, and how beautiful, and how much he loved you."

Dennis' fingers closed finally about the handle of the poker. He tensed, watching for the right moment to move.

"That weekend you came up here," Frank went on, raving like a madman, unaware of Dennis' intentions, "I realized what a golden opportunity it was for me. I had set up others the same way, taking pictures of them while they had sex. In the beginning, the pictures were only for my own pleasure; but when Linc asked about bringing you up here for

146

a weekend, I saw that I could make lots of money, and I could ruin Linc Gardner anytime I wanted, and you too. It was a chance I couldn't afford to pass up. I spent most of one night outside that bedroom, taking picture after picture, and half-freezing to death, but it was worth the effort. If Linc hadn't been so foolish, I would have made a nice fortune off of him, I planned to bleed him for months, and later on, you as well."

"You've made every penny you'll ever make off those pictures," Dennis said, jerking his head in the direction of the fireplace. "They're gone, every single one of them, in ashes."

Frank's face turned grim and angry again. "Yes, you've ruined that for me," he said, "but I don't care, it was still worth it. Lincoln Gardner is gone, and you will be too. And I can always take more pictures. There are always plenty of fools out there, they get horny and they stop using their brains, a perfect situation for a clever man like me."

Dennis waited tensely. Frank's eyes had never left him, and the gun was still pointed directly at him. It would take only a fraction of a second for him to squeeze the trigger; less time, certainly, that it would take to leap across the few feet that separated them and wield the poker; but it was the only chance he had.

"Jeff is gone, too," Dennis said. "I would say you've been pretty busy lately."

"Him?" Frank sneered. "He was nothing, an animal. I even went to his filthy apartment, it was a different apartment then, but just as shabby, and I had sex with him, to convince him to help me. It was disgusting, that enormous tool of his, that hairy body, even his buttocks were covered with hair, like some great shaggy dog, and the things he wanted me to do to please him, and I did them, because I needed his help, and all I could think of the entire time I was doing them was how much I wanted to kill him. I did the world a service by getting rid of him. I didn't find your note until later, but I knew when I saw you leaving his apartment that I would have to do something about him. I had already decided to before that, but of course I needed your help in finding him once he had disappeared. I'm grateful to you for that."

"What did you do, trick him the way you did Linc?" Dennis asked. "It seems to me that Jeff would have been a pretty rough customer."

"He was a fool. He was actually glad to see me. Can you imagine that?" Frank laughed aloud. "He even suggested that we have sex again. He invited me to perform those same disgusting services for him, he really thought that he could give me pleasure by allowing me to perform them on him, he thought by making me happy that way he could persuade me afterward to give myself up and confess everything. You must have given him quite a lecture about doing the right thing. But then, you do have persuasive charms."

Dennis felt a sense of relief that Frank had not been in time to witness the sex between himself and Jeff. He had provided Frank with more than enough perverted entertainment; but that was small comfort in his present predicament.

"Did you shoot him before you threw him out the window?" he asked, still working for time.

"Oh, no, nothing that bothersome—someone might have heard the gunshot. The fool went to look out the window, I actually think he was watching you, I think he desired you, and while he was turned away from me, I hit him on the back of the head with a lamp. I poured a couple of beers over him, dragged him to the window, and gave him a hard shove. I had hoped that the fall would disguise the blow to his head, but as luck would have it, the police saw that right off."

"Do you know," Dennis said softly, trying to find a way to divert Frank's attention, "There's one sad element to all this: you came very close to having the sort of lover Linc had, the very same lover, in fact. I had become very fond of you since Linc's death. You were absolutely right, Frank. In time, I would probably have gone to bed with you, even if it had only been out of gratitude. I felt I owed it to you."

The gun wavered for a second. "Yes, of course, I had that in mind for us," Frank said. "I wanted you badly. That, at least, wasn't an act. And that would have been the ultimate triumph for me, to steal you away from Linc, even in death. It was hell, you know, watching you that night as I took those pictures. You are beautiful when you're naked, especially when you are aroused and making love. I don't know why you had so much difficulty deciding upon your homosexuality. You were born to give a man pleasure."

Dennis forced himself to smile up at the older man. "I've grown since then," he said, in the most seductive voice he could manage. "Since that night you watched us, and took the pictures. You should see me now, Frank."

The gun was growing increasingly unsteady. Frank's tongue licked hungrily at his lips. Dennis knew what he was contemplating, and the thought filled him with dread, but it was the only way he could think of to get Frank off guard.

"Wouldn't you like to see me naked again," he asked, still smiling. "And aroused? While I'm still alive, still able to give a man pleasure? There isn't much pleasure in making love to a corpse."

"You are bluffing," Frank snapped, growing increasingly nervous. "You think you can talk me out of killing you, but you are mistaken."

Dennis let go of the poker. He would never be able to get across the room to use that before Frank shot him. There was only one other weapon he had to use: his body. "It can't hurt anything to have a look, can it?" he asked persuasively. Slowly, careful not to alarm Frank, he stood. His legs were stiff from crouching for so long, but he forced himself to stand erect and steady.

"Don't try anything funny," Frank warned him, brandishing the gun.

Dennis said nothing. He smiled and began slowly to unbutton his shirt. Never in his life had he felt less inclined toward anything to do with sex; but sex was the best weapon he had now, the only weapon, particularly against a perverted mind like Frank's. Surely Frank would be unable to resist the idea of seeing him totally naked.

He dropped the shirt to the floor and, ever so slowly, peeled his T-shirt upward, over his head, baring his well-defined chest with its little copper penny nipples, not knowing for sure if the gun might go off at any moment.

Nude from the waist up, he kicked his loafers off his feet and stooped to remove his stockings one at a time. It was working; he was sure of it. Frank's eyes were glued to his hands, watching them reveal more and more naked skin.

He paused for long minute, fully conscious of the golden gleam that the firelight gave his body. "Want me to go on, Frank?" he asked.

"Take them off," Frank said hoarsely, waving a hand toward his jeans.

With the same deliberate, maddeningly slow movements, Dennis unfastened his belt, unbuttoned his fly, and pushed his jeans downward, over his hips, letting them drop to the floor. He stepped out of them, clad now only in a pair of tight briefs that merely served to accentuate his natural endowments.

Frank stared bug-eyed at the well-filled shorts, his expression wild with anticipation. His breath was rapid and uneven, his hands trembling. His trousers swelled outward in front.

Dennis hooked his thumbs in the band of elastic at his waist. "Do you want to take them off, Frank?" he asked in a whisper, "Or shall I?"

Frank took a step forward, then checked himself. "You do it," he ordered in a strained voice.

Dennis rolled the short slowly downward, over his hips. Frank's excitement was mounting. He gasped aloud as the glowing firelight stuck the lush tangle of golden silk, and a moment later, the column of delectable flesh it cushioned.

Dennis stepped out of the shorts as well. He was completely naked now, a visual feast of male beauty. He stood motionless, allowing Frank's eyes to devour him inch by inch, drinking in the sight before him.

"You've never touched me, Frank," he crooned softly. "You've never known just what my body feels like. My skin is very soft and smooth. Linc used to say it was like caressing velvet. Wouldn't you like to feel me, all of me, touch the velvet? Wouldn't you like to taste me, just one time? Linc used to say it was the sweetest one he had ever tasted. Why don't you find that out for yourself?"

It was now or never, he thought. Frank was beside himself with desire, scarcely able to hold the gun in his shaking hand, the fabric of his trousers straining outward with his excitement.

His heart in his throat, Dennis took a slow step forward, and another. He cupped himself in one hand, lifted it toward Frank as if offering him a gift. "For you, Frank," he said, fondling himself to make it begin to grow. Slowly it stretched in length, rising into the air as it stiffened. "Delicious, he used to say. Sweeter than candy."

Frank reached out as if he were hypnotized. His hand brushed the velvet flesh of one lean hip, and he reached for the golden treasure being offered to him. Dennis waited until the trembling fingers touched his turgid manhood—and then he lunged.

The gun fired aimlessly before it fell from Frank's hand and landed with a clatter on the floor. Frank fell backward, taking Dennis down with him.

It was like wrestling with a wild bear. His youth and his lack of clothes to hinder him gave Dennis an advantage in speed and agility, but Frank was a man of enormous weight and brute strength. Dennis found himself caught in a crushing embrace that drove the breath from his lungs.

He fought wildly, trying to break the grip that Frank had on him. They rolled, knocking over a chair and a little table as they went, the rough surface of the wooden floor scraping against Dennis' naked flesh.

He managed to break free and dived for the gun, but Frank was upon him again before he could get it, pinning him to the floor with sheer weight. A crushing blow from his fist knocked Dennis' head sideways, and he felt the room spinning about him. His strength was fading fast. Unless he could reach the gun, or some weapon, he was done for.

He rolled free, but Frank landed a savage kick into his crotch. Dennis doubled over with a cry of agony, and Frank delivered another sledgehammer blow to his chin. Dennis lunged sideways, dodging yet another kick, and half jumped, half crawled toward the poker. He was too late, however; before he could grab for it, Frank had retrieved the gun.

"Don't try it," Frank said.

Dennis had one glimpse of the gun, once more aimed at him, and then from nowhere, it seemed, there was someone else in the room with them, a streak of leather hurling itself at Frank.

154

CHAPTER TWELVE
◊

Dennis stared in astonishment as Sandy and Frank grappled with one another. It was almost impossible to believe his eyes. Sandy, here, in the cabin with them? It was like a miracle out of the blue.

Frank was already tired, and Sandy, tall and beefy himself, was more of a match for him than Dennis had been. Dennis took advantage of the opportunity to retrieve the gun from the floor, just in case. Then he stood back and let them fight it out.

The fight was over in a few minutes. Frank crumpled under the powerful blows Sandy rained on him, and finally he sank to the floor, unconscious.

Panting, but with a smile on his face, Sandy rose from his fallen opponent and turned toward Dennis, his eyes going up and down the naked loveliness before him.

Dennis blushed and laughed. "If you had been a few minutes faster," he said, coming into the arms Sandy opened for him, "I'd have still had my clothes on."

"Are you kidding?" Sandy asked, kissing him quickly and hugging the naked body to his own. "I've got a right to see what I'm fighting for, it seems to me. Besides, I almost didn't make it at all. I lost you once on the road coming up here, and drove around for a while before I saw him coming out of a store down the way, and then I lost him again coming back, and had to look around some more until I finally spotted his tracks coming up this lane, and followed them, and found you."

He stepped back and looked at Dennis more seriously. "What the hell are you doing in the raw, anyway?" he asked. "Did that bastard...?"

Dennis shook his head. "No, but thank God he wanted to. I was doing my Dance of the Seven Veils to try to distract him, until I could think of something better to do. If I must say so myself, though, you missed a pretty good strip show."

"With luck, maybe I can get a private showing," Sandy said.

They kissed again, longer and harder. "I think we had better save that show for another time, however," Sandy said when they finally separated. He gave Dennis' bare rump and slap. "Come on, lover, we had better get out of this place before he wakes up. I don't need any more exercise this morning, thank you."

Dennis glanced down at the unconscious man on the floor. "Shouldn't we take him with us?" he asked.

"In the MG?" Sandy said. "There's hardly room for him, if you'll recall. Besides, I'd just as soon leave him for the rats. We'll call the police when we get to a phone, and tell them where he is."

"You're the boss," Dennis said, happy to let Sandy take charge. He started toward the door.

"Just be sure you remember that," Sandy said. "And, uh, by the way, don't you think you're forgetting something?"

Dennis stopped and looked back, and realized as he met Sandy's amused gaze, that he was still naked. "Guess I was at that," he said with a laugh.

He dressed considerably faster than he had undressed earlier. Grabbing his bag at last, he took Sandy's arm and they left together. Not until they were down the lane and on the road, however, did he really begin to breathe easily.

"I guess I owe you one hell of an apology," he said finally. "If it's any consolation, I wanted to tell you the truth all along, but I was afraid…oh, hell, you may as well know the worst: I thought you were the one who killed Lincoln Gardner."

"You were his lover, weren't you?" Sandy asked as he drove.

"You knew that?" Dennis asked, surprised.

"It took me a while to figure it out, although I should have known after that first night with you. I knew you looked familiar, but I didn't connect you to those pictures at first. Even that apartment I drove you to—that was Gardner's apartment, wasn't it?"

"Yes, I've been staying there while I was in town. Our families are old friends."

"I should have put two and two together," Sandy said, "But I just wasn't thinking clearly, not even when you pulled that stunt with the names. I had Jeff on my mind, and I was worried about how to get him out of the jam he was in. It wasn't until after he caught you going through my dresser that I began to suspect you were up to something."

"But you continued to see me," Dennis said.

Sandy glanced sideways at him, grinning. "Has it occurred to you I might have had a good reason for that? Like, a good *hard* reason? Or maybe two hard ones?"

Dennis blushed and laughed, and reached over to rest one hand on a muscular thigh. Sandy reached down to cover the hand with his own.

"I'm sorry about Jeff," Dennis said softly. "I feel that I was partly to blame for what happened to him. If it hadn't been for me…"

"Don't blame yourself. I hated to have it happen, too, but with a guy like Jeff, it was bound to happen some day. He was always playing with fire. This time, he got himself all mixed up in a blackmail scheme. Even if he didn't know the details, he knew enough to know that what he was doing was wrong."

"How did you find us up here, anyway?" Dennis asked. "Did you follow us from my place?"

"Yep, I knew you were there, at the apartment, and just not answering the door. And I knew you had been at Jeff's place earlier. When you didn't show up at The Ship's Call, I got to thinking, and I thought some more about those pictures. Your hair was different, and your face, nobody's face looks exactly the same when they are doing the things you were doing in those photos, but there was one thing I should have recognized immediately, considering how often I had right in front of my face.

"As soon as I remembered that, I tumbled to the fact that it was you with Gardner, and I knew what you were up to, and what you must have thought. I headed for Jeff's right away. I wanted to set you straight; I knew if you had realized he was involved with Gardner's death, you must think I had been too. I couldn't stand the thought that you might believe that about me. But I got to Jeff's too late. He was already dead, and you had been seen leaving his place. I knew you had to be next on the murderer's list, so I headed for Gardner's apartment. When you didn't answer the door, I parked down the street and waited. And as soon as I saw you leave with that creep, I knew he was the one. I recognized him from the bar, the night he and Jeff had their heads together plotting. Of course, I didn't know then what it was they were plotting."

"Thank god you saw us, and followed," Dennis said.

"I guess I wasn't very honest with you, either," Sandy said. "But I think we can both understand. I just hope in the future we can work things out a little better."

"We will," Dennis said. He smiled happily. Sandy had forgiven him and wanted him for a lover. It was more than he could have hoped for.

The long hours without sleep were weighing heavily on him, however. The MG had no top, and the mountain air was nippy, but the seats sat down low on the floor, and the windshield deflected most of the crisp cold air up and over their heads. With the car's heater blasting warm air at them, it was actually kind of cozy. He closed his eyes and leaned back against the seat, enjoying the feel of Sandy's muscular thigh under his hand and the purr of the sport car's engine.

"Damn!" Sandy swore aloud and suddenly speeded up, taking the next curve with squealing tires.

Startled, Dennis sat upright. "What's wrong?" he asked when he saw Sandy's grim expression.

"I guess you were right," Sandy said, "We should have done something with that joker, tied him up, maybe."

Dennis glanced back in time to see a glimpse of Frank's Caddy only a short stretch behind them. It disappeared from sight as they rounded another curve, and then appeared again, even closer.

"Better hang on," Sandy said, flinging the MG around still another sharp curve. "This is going to get rough."

Sandy had been driving leisurely up until now, and they didn't have much of a lead over Frank. The Cadillac was perhaps a hundred yards behind, and gaining on them on every straight stretch, the Detroit monster's sheer weight giving it the edge on a downhill race. Sandy glanced anxiously at the tiny rearview mirror on the MG's dashboard.

At least, Frank had his hands full back there. Sandy knew that the Cadillac handled like a bathtub on wheels. Its mushy suspension, passenger-coddling shocks, the soft seat with no lateral support for the driver, and its huge, under inflated tires all made for a cloud like ride on the open highway, but they also made it less than road-worthy, especially on a twisting, turning road like this one. Sandy's only hope was to use his car's better handling to his advantage. If Frank ever got close enough to pull alongside them, it wouldn't take more than a bump from that monster to send the little MG plummeting over the sheer drop-off beside the road.

They roared through turn after turn, tires screaming in protest, Sandy using the gears to slow them as they approached the turns and to accelerate out of them as fast as possible. The MG's engine sounded like a cloud of angry hornets. Sandy wished the car were a little younger, an MGB, say. The newer models had disc brakes and a bit more of an engine. Right now he could use all the help he could get.

In the mirror, he saw the hood of the Caddy yaw and pitch this way and that, Frank fighting it all the way, power-sliding into curves and wrestling it through the tightest places by sheer, brute force.

Still, he was doing well enough to stay on the road, and to continue to gain on them, and Sandy knew it was only a matter of time before he was breathing down their necks. What then? There weren't that many places where he could pull along-side without risking a head on collision with anyone going in the other direction—but Frank was proba-bly not in his right mind, and he might not even consider that danger.

The road wound its way sharply down the mountain. To the side, Dennis could look down into a wide valley, and he shuddered as he imagined them flying off the road and dropping into that dis-tant vale of green. He looked back and saw Frank's Cadillac even closer, no more than fifty yards away.

The tires shrieked in protest as they slid pre-cariously around each curve, a fender once actually touching the guardrail at the edge of the road and sending sparks flying. The motor whined each time Sandy accelerated. The MG gained a few feet with each turn, but the Caddy ate it back up with each straightaway.

The road straightened out and began another sharp descent. Sandy crushed the accelerator to the floor, running it flat out, the engine screaming. The pine trees and the rocky crags and the dizzying vistas shot past at a blurring speed. Ahead of them, Dennis saw a sign warning of a sharp bend to the left. By the time he had blinked, they were past the warning sign. Sandy slammed the stick forward, into a lower gear. The MG skidded at breakneck speed and there was a crunch of metal as they hit the guardrail again, harder than before, knocking Dennis sideways in his seat. Then they were around, and on the straightaway again.

He looked over his shoulder. Behind them, the Caddy leaned almost on it side, but somehow Frank managed to barrel around the curve. They had gained a few yards on him but they were once again losing them as the Cadillac edged closer and closer, close enough now that Dennis could see Frank through the windshield, grinning demonically, and bent over the wheel as he drew up to them and pulled out into the left lane to go alongside.

Sandy swerved, trying to keep him back. The fenders brushed and the MG lurched out of control. Sandy righted it, but it had given Frank his opportunity. The Cadillac was beside them now, forcing them over toward the cliff on their right.

Ahead of them, the road veered sharply to the left again. Directly before them was a panorama of valleys and mountains, sweeping nearer and nearer. Dennis stared ahead in fascinated horror. The Cadillac was forcing them over to the edge, to the cliff. Even if they could somehow get past it, they could never hope to make that curve at the speed they were traveling. Either way, they were going over.

He was thrown suddenly forward, his head banging against the windshield, as Sandy slammed on the brakes and shifted down to help them stop.

Unprepared for this maneuver, Frank shot past them. The MG squealed and skidded, turning crazily about in the roadway. There was a loud crash of metal on metal, and for a second or two Dennis thought they were going over the edge.

As the MG shuddered to a stop, he realized that it was the Caddy he had heard, smashing through the guardrail. He could still hear it as it crashed and rolled downward, into the valley below.

They sat limp and speechless for a long moment, neither of them quite able to grasp that they had escaped with their lives.

"I guess we won't have to worry about him," Sandy said finally. "No one could live through that."

"Could he have made that curve?" Dennis asked breathlessly. "Or do you think…?"

"There's no way he could have made it," Sandy said. "Not at that speed, in that car. We'd never have made it either. I had to take a chance on stopping. I guess these brakes are better than I thought."

Dennis had begun to cry, for reasons he was not quite sure of himself. "I think I need to stretch my legs," he said wearily, starting to open the door.

Sandy grabbed for him, holding tight to his arm, and nodded toward the side of the car. Dennis looked out and jumped back. They were on the actual edge, no more than an inch or two of ground separating them from the same fate Frank had suffered.

The engine had stalled. Sandy started it up and edged the car cautiously forward, away from the precipice. He stopped on the highway again.

"Still want to stretch your legs?" he asked, racing the motor.

Dennis shook his ash-white face. "I think I'll wait till we're down the hill," he said when he could manage to get words out again.

Sandy leaned across the seat and took him in his arms, and kissed him ardently. Then he laughed, and put the car in gear, and started to drive once more.

Dennis averted his eyes as they drove past the spot where Frank had gone through the guardrail.

* * * * * *

"Flight two thirty-six, for New York City, now boarding at Gate Number Seven," a bored voice announced over the loudspeakers in the waiting room.

With a sigh, Dennis dropped his cigarette into an ash receptacle, crushing it out. "Guess I've put it off as long as I can," he said. "If I don't want trouble with the Navy, I'd better catch this plane."

"We don't want trouble with the Navy," Sandy said. "Or anyone else for that matter. Come on, I'll walk you to the gate."

The lines of passengers were already forming at the boarding gate as they neared it.

"Funny, it seems like such a long time ago when I landed here," Dennis said thoughtfully. "And started all of this for us. I knew when I left for Los Angeles that it was going to be a difficult journey, but I never dreamed it would turn out the way it did."

"It's too bad about Linc," Sandy said quietly. He paused a few feet from the other passengers. "He must have been a great guy. I can imagine how you must have felt, arriving here, and learning about his murder."

Dennis smiled sadly. "It's only fair to tell you that I still think about him a lot, and I miss him. I probably always will. But that's something different from what I feel for you. I can't explain it any better than that, but the love I feel for you is different from what I felt for him. That doesn't have to stand in our way."

"It won't," Sandy said. "Don't even worry about that."

"It's strange, but when Linc used to tell me that he loved me, I couldn't believe him. Then, I didn't think it was possible for two people of the same sex to be really in love with one another."

"And now?" Sandy's eyes were expectant and hopeful.

"Now," Dennis said, his own eyes filled with affection, "I know better."

The other passengers were disappearing down the ramp to the plane. Sandy looked deep into his eyes, and his lips formed the words that he couldn't say aloud: goodbye, my lover.

With a final shake of hands and a look that said more than words could ever convey, they parted. Dennis hurried down the ramp without once looking back, though he knew Sandy still stood where he had been, watching him go.

Once on the plane, Dennis found a seat by himself and fastened his seat belt. Closing his eyes, he thought back over the past weeks, thinking of all that had happened to him since he arrived at this same airport. He thought of Linc, and Linc's murder, and all that had followed in its wake.

Jeff had died too, and then Frank. Even Frank's death saddened him somewhat, despite the fact that Frank had tried to kill him. Poor Frank. His entire life had been a lie, pretending to himself that he had a talent he didn't possess, pretending to be Linc's friend. If only he had met someone, the right someone, before he had gone so far down that road to madness.

Dennis had spent a great deal of time with Sergeant Mathews after Frank's death. Eventually, Mathews had put together enough evidence to support the story Dennis had given him. There were still pictures in Frank's apartment, and in his haste to go after them, Frank had left his gun at the cabin and ballistics tests had confirmed that it was the weapon that had killed Linc.

For whatever reasons of his own, Mathews had done all that he could to play down the homosexual aspect of the murders, and so spared them a scandal, for which Dennis was grateful. Mathews had even, in fact, insisted that Dennis look him up when he got back into town, and Dennis had wondered with a smile if perhaps there wasn't a little more than "understanding" involved in Mathews' kindness. He had promised, however, that he would indeed look the policeman up, and Sandy had seconded the invitation.

"You live here in L.A.?" a voice asked near him, breaking into Dennis' thoughts.

He stared surprised at the speaker. He had been so engrossed in his thoughts he had not even been aware that anyone had taken the vacant seat beside him.

"No," he said, smiling, "I was just here for a visit."

"Nice city," the stranger said, nodding toward the view of Los Angeles below them as they soared upward into the air. "I hope you plan to come back again sometime."

Dennis stared out the window at the city, spreading now for miles beneath them, seemingly endless. "Yes, I certainly do," he said, more to himself than to the stranger.

I will be coming back, he promised himself silently, as he had promised Sandy only a short while before. And the next time he arrived here, there would be none of the questions and the doubts in his mind about the man he was going to meet. He would be coming back to his lover.

My lover. He said the words over again to himself, and decided he liked them.

ABOUT THE AUTHOR
◇

Lecturer, former writing instructor and early rabble-rouser for gay rights and freedom of the press, **VIC-TOR J. BANIS** is the critically acclaimed author ("...a master storyteller"—*Publishers Weekly*) of more than 140 published novels and nonfiction works, and his verse and short pieces have appeared in numerous journals (*Blithe House Quarterly*, Fall 2006) and anthologies (*Charmed Lives*, Lethe Press, 2006).